An Eastern Seduction

Our lives are completed when we love fully, passionately, eternally, unconditionally.
—without doubt or reservation– appreciating love as the most courageous of acts!

An Eastern Seduction

by

Rebecca Rosenblat

Commonwealth
Publications

A Commonwealth Publications Paperback
AN EASTERN SEDUCTION

This edition published 1996
by Commonwealth Publications
9764 - 45th Avenue,
Edmonton, AB, CANADA T6E 5C5
All rights reserved
Copyright © 1995 by Rebecca Rosenblat

ISBN: 1-55197-519-X

Printed in Canada
Designed by: Jennifer Brolsma

To Henry, Goedy, Joshy, and Davy for believing in me and supporting me unconditionally.

ACKNOWLEDGEMENT

Many thanks to Patrick for his loyal support.

CHAPTER ONE

Jake knew it was going to be a long hot summer. Record high temperatures had already begun to cast their suffocating spell across the continents. Trees drooped from fatigue and exhaustion, unable to breathe air into the dreadfully stifling nights. The slightest aberration—a dripping faucet, a buzzing fly—provoked enough commotion to choke sleep, agitate senses and fray tempers. Law records the world over registered that similar heatwaves had been responsible for inciting random acts of violence.

Unaware of the terror poised to lacerate his being, Jake tossed and turned on his cool satin sheets, a thin film of perspiration covering his body.

Suddenly, the chimes in his window started an erotic dance. A gentle breeze blew the lace curtains against the silvery shells that glistened in the light of the full moon. Their hypnotic tingle finally lulled Jake into a fitful sleep.

There she was again, teasing and torturing him in his dreams. He had never met the woman, but she embodied everything he had ever wanted. She was perfect, a figment of his imagination and every man's fantasy. Jake felt his pelvis tingle and tighten as he envisioned her gracefully gliding toward him, her outstretched arms reaching for him. A sheer dress clung revealingly to her sweltering body. Her shiny raven tresses bounced by the sides of her face, framing her gray eyes and delicate nose. Her full lips quivered and parted invitingly. The fire in Jake's groin intensified as he hungrily thrust out his arms to grab her. But she disappeared before he could take her, just as she had done a thousand times before.

Jake sat bolt upright in bed, bathed in a cold sweat. It was becoming a nightly ritual for him. A part of him looked forward to her visits, but his body only ached from unfulfilled desire. He shouted, "Who are you, and why are you doing this to me? You're robbing me of my sleep and my sanity... Damn it, why can't I get you out of my mind?"

Jake walked over to the armoire and looked at himself in the mirror above it. He slammed his right fist into his left palm. "Imagine, *moi*, Jake Alexander, bachelor of the year, talking to an illusion. The *Queens' Tribune* would just love to get a hold of this one."

It was almost morning. The soothing chimes and velvety breeze were back on strike, the trees that fanned them motionless once again. Jake put on his boxer shorts and decided to go for a run through Blossom Park. He knew that he needed an invigorating jog since sleep would not come again.

* * * *

As he ran, Jake planned out his day at the hospital. He looked forward to wrapping up surgery by late morning, spending a relaxed afternoon doing consultations in his office, then cutting out early. It would give him a chance to join Hans for that long overdue drink.

Jake briefly wondered whether or not to mention his nightly problem to Hans. Being a psychiatrist, Hans was certainly capable of offering a professional interpretation of the recurrent dream. But as a friend, he would more than likely start reintroducing him to every female from the health club, just as he had done before when Sharon had left, and, subsequently, when he was selected bachelor of the year. Jake laughed at the memory of the singles scene Hans had immersed him into.

It helped him decide against declaring his desire and lust for his elusive dream-girl.

As he completed his run around the final curve, Jake glanced back over his shoulder to take in the breathtaking view of the rolling hillside. It was blanketed with a patchwork of flowers set against the pinkish backdrop of dawn. Jake nicknamed it 'Wordsworth Hill' in honor of the poem *Daffodils*. When Jake swung his head around this time, a familiar silhouette nearly knocked him off balance.

This has got to stop. Now she is invading my days—making any woman that even slightly resembles her give me the creeps.

Jake showered, changed and raced out his red RX-7 to mingle in with the flow of traffic heading downtown. As always, he weaved through, breaking a few speed laws here and there.

He glanced at his Rolex, smiled to himself and signaled to make a turn into the doctors' parking. To his amazement, he could have sworn he saw his dream-girl enter the hospital through the main entrance.

Jake shook his head and said, "My mind really *has* started playing tricks on me. Meeting one of Hans' shapely friends may not be such a bad idea after all."

At five o'clock, Jake met Hans at their favorite pub, across the street from the hospital. Although it still had all the ingredients that made it their preferred watering hole—pool tables, jukebox, comfy chairs, intricate Tiffany lamps and familiar patrons—something was missing for Jake.

Looking at his million-mile-away blank stare, Hans asked Jake, "What's the matter, big guy? You've been nursing the same martini all evening."

"It's just somebody who I can't seem to get out of my mind."

"Must be quite the lady to hold your attention like that. In all the years I have known you, no one except Sharon ever occupied your mind long enough to even get a second date. And since her, you seemed to have sworn off women altogether."

"Stop teasing, Hans. It's not funny... I think I'll call it a night. We'll try this again another time. And maybe next time we can even double with a couple of your friends from the club."

"*The* Jake Alexander wants *me* to fix him up with someone? She must have really broken your heart!"

Three nights went by. Jake's dream-girl stopped coming to him, titillating his desire. He felt uncomfortable missing her. But then his predicament worsened—she began occupying more and more of his daydreams. It was as if she had boldly stepped out of his nights into his days.

Indeed, she had. Jake almost bumped into her as he stopped the hospital elevator by slipping his hand between the shutting doors and sliding his body into it. Her gaze pierced through him as she stared at him shamelessly. Jake wondered if he was dreaming.

Never before had he seen her up close. Bravely, Jake took a step toward her to make room for one more person in the already packed-beyond-capacity elevator. The brush of her warm skin assured him that she was very real this time.

As the doors opened to the seventh floor, Jake couldn't help but follow her out. "Have we met before? I feel like I know you from somewhere."

"How original. Do women still buy lines like that these days?"

"I'm sorry, I didn't mean to sound like a pick-up artist, least of all in a place like this... Your face really has come to me before. I just can't seem to pinpoint where... I apologize if I've embarrassed you."

"Look, mister, I'm sure we've never met. I'm not one to forget a face. And as flattered as I am, I'm not interested... I'm here to see my husband. He has been disabled in a terrible car accident."

"I'm sorry to hear that."

After an awkward pause, Jake continued, "I didn't realize that you're married. Since I didn't see a wedding ring, I just assumed—"

"That I was fair game? No, mister, having a husband generally means unavailable—in my book, anyway."

"I apologize, Mrs....?"

"Fairchild. Samantha Fairchild."

Jake extended his right hand to shake hers. "I'm Jake Alexander. I'm on staff here. If you need anything, please don't hesitate to locate me through information. It will be my way of showing I can be a gentleman," Jake smiled.

Having shook hands, Samantha stood still, inspecting Jake. Her keen observation of his tall, muscular form and chiseled face showed definite signs of interest on her part.

Not knowing what to say, Jake walked away—feeling cheated out of his fantasy. Although Samantha was every bit as beautiful as the vision that filled his nights with passion, her demeanor left a lot to be desired. Her soft husky voice was enticing, but her sarcasm and blatant glare were a turn-off.

"Never mind that," Jake thought aloud. "I have got to figure out where I saw her before all those dreams started. I just know I had to have seen her somewhere. There can be no other logical explanation for a real life duplicate of a dream-girl... But where?"

Another week flew by without Jake seeing his dream-girl, or Samantha Fairchild. The mystery of the whole situation and his preoccupation with a married woman was very unsettling to him. But since he couldn't just let it go, he decided to give fate a helping hand.

Friday after work, Jake paid a visit to Mr. Fairchild's room, hoping to run into his lovely wife. Samantha walked in just as he had wished, looking more exquisite than all of his fantasies. Being totally taken by her, he ogled, without a word of greeting. Fortunately for him, Mr. Fairchild still appeared to be fast asleep.

"I hope you don't mind that I came to check in on your husband. We haven't had a chance to talk yet, though... He's been in a deep sleep."

"He rarely opens his eyes. As for talking—it's been weeks since he has said a word, even though he is biologically capable of it, from what I've been told... The doctors feel he is severely depressed. I guess I would be too, if I were that helpless."

"Must be very difficult for you."

"More than you could possibly imagine." Having said that, Samantha became detached from the here and now. Her distracted glare and strained expression made it obvious that there was a lot more to the story.

Jake tried to interject. "May I buy you dinner?"

Samantha smiled, checked her imaginary calendar, and said, "You're lucky, Dr. Alexander, I just got a cancellation. I think I could squeeze you in... How does seven sound?"

"Seven sounds great. Meet you by the main entrance." Jake's stomach tightened with a nervousness that generally accompanies a first date—not being able to distinguish between a dream come true or the illicitness of the anticipated deed.

CHAPTER TWO

Jake selected the noisy King of Snapper for his date to end all dates. The loud clanging of colliding pots, pans and dishes in the kitchen competed with the dining room hum of chatting clientele. Glaring fluorescent lighting and a large sports television further depleted any hints of coziness. The place seemed to be custom-tailored for discouraging intimacy. Jake felt it was perfect, since Samantha was a married woman with a disabled husband lying in a hospital bed a mere two blocks away. Jake was convinced that striking up a friendship with an obviously distracted lady would put his sensual cravings for her to rest—once and for all—allowing him to return to his normal life.

Jake ordered up a carafe of white house wine, and they leisurely looked through their menus. Having made their selections, they began talking. To Jake's surprise, the conversation took on a flirtatious tone, despite his limiting himself to general questions.

Through dinner, Jake learned that Samantha was a political science teacher, who also happened to possess an eclectic knowledge of world history and art. Her wit impressed him almost as much as her sensuality. She reminded him of Sharon, with the exception of her genuine compassion for the less fortunate—something his ex-wife's selfish nature could never comprehend. Jake was completely taken by her.

As the evening drew to an end, Jake swallowed the last piece of his coffee cake and said, "They sure didn't make teachers like you in my day."

Samantha broke out into hearty laughter, shaking her head in disbelief. "You sure have a way with trite lines, Dr. Alexander."

Jake got up from his chair, leaned across the table to take Samantha's chin in his hand, and tilted up her face. "My gosh! My diagnosis was accurate. The lady can actually laugh."

Before Samantha could answer, a blinding flash snapped a picture of their innocently compromising pose.

"Who the hell was that? Is your husband having you followed to make sure you're behaving in his absence?"

"Not very likely. Why would he? We were never..."

"What were you going to say?"

"Nothing that I wish to discuss... Would you mind taking me home now, or call me a cab if it is too much out of your way."

There it was again—an elusiveness around the circumstances of her marriage. It mystified Jake. But what he found to be even more intriguing was his preoccupation with her—since he could have his pick of any number of more receptive and available women.

The morning paper published a picture of the infamous Dr. Alexander with the lovely Mrs. Fairchild. Who could have done something like that? It was a cheap tabloid in the society pages, designed to discredit the fine doctor's reputation. Allegations ranged from taking advantage of a married woman's vulnerability to a possible mix-up in Far East politics!

As appalled as Jake was at reading the cheap and inaccurate piece of trash—with a good mind to file a lawsuit—he worried more for Samantha Fairchild and the trouble it could cause her with her husband.

Despite the early hour, Jake decided to take the paper to her home, to prepare her for any unexpected consequences. He felt he owed it to her, since he was certain the publicity was on his account.

Having rung the doorbell a few times, Jake waited impatiently for an answer. Samantha finally opened the door in a flimsy satin robe. Jake marched in without a word, ignoring the puzzled expression on her face. Securing her door shut, he handed her the distasteful article.

"I think you had better take a look at this before you go to visit your husband."

Samantha skimmed through the article while Jake looked around at her living room. Morning rays joined the bright orange *dhuri* on the floor, bathing the room with a salmon hue. Brass vases with colorful inlays glinted on the mantle. Their arresting tones complemented the beaded, embroidered mural that hung behind them, depicting a love scene.

Jake's inventory of the East Indian artifacts was interrupted by a whisper. "Oh my gosh, they've found us."

"Who are they? I ask you again, has your husband hired people to follow you and keep tabs on your whereabouts? I demand to know."

Before Samantha could address Jake, her doorbell started to ring again—incessantly. Samantha began trembling, and chose not to answer.

"Aren't you going to get that?"

"No, Jake, I'm afraid."

"Of what—an innocent dinner?"

"Don't ask me anymore. I don't want you involved in any of this."

"I think it's a little too late for that. You already seem to have landed me in the middle of whatever this is."

"I insisted on wanting to be left alone, but your

ego couldn't take 'no' for an answer! So in a moment of weakness, I decided to go along with you. I—"

The conversation was interrupted by a thunderous knock at the door.

"Open up, Mrs. Fairchild. This is the police."

"Police? Look, Mrs. Fairchild, I may be new to the game, but the last time I checked, buying dinner for a married woman was hardly against the law! I intend to open that door right now and prove my innocence in whatever it is you are involved in."

Without checking for Samantha's approval, Jake walked to the door and swung it open. Two policeman, a journalist, and a plainclothes detective or perhaps even a secret agent—judging by his expensive threads—made their way abruptly into Samantha's little townhouse.

This was the second time in less than twelve hours that cameras started to flash in Jake Alexander's face—this time more intimidatingly than before.

Samantha finally gathered enough courage in her tremulous voice to ask, "What is going on?"

"As if you didn't know! You had better get a picture of her feigned reaction when we do our bit to give her the news. It might come in handy," the plainclothesman instructed the journalist with the camera.

Finding the camera in position, the stouter of the two policemen cleared his throat—in preparation for his speech—and stepped forward. His smug expression testified to his confidence and the enjoyment of his job.

"Here goes... Mrs. Fairchild, your husband—Mr. Norman Fairchild—was murdered a couple of hours ago. He died of asphyxiation, suffocated by a pillow in his hospital bed. *Now*, do either one of you have something to tell us?"

Samantha's face displayed shock, fear and a sense of relief. She stood speechless.

Jake's face, on the other hand, felt hot with horror and disgust. The last few days had been bizarre enough, with his dream-girl stepping into his real world. And now—with Norman Fairchild's murder—his very wish for the obstacle which stood between them to disappear had come true... *Who is this woman who has violated my life in a curious way, and dragged me into an unusual and eccentric world?* Jake realized that his life was not going to be the same again. The unknown stirred him up, as did the invigorating thought of living on the edge with a mysterious woman.

The conversations in the room were nothing but a loud blur to Jake, until he was personally addressed by the rotund officer.

"Doesn't look good for you, buddy. First you are seen dining with the lady the night before her husband is killed. Then you are seen leaving with her. And now, you're in her home in the early morning, with her looking like that—a couple of hours after her old man's been popped."

"I resent your implications. I just got here a few minutes before you guys, for an entirely different matter. I know nothing of this. Who would want to kill a disabled man is completely beyond me. As for Mrs. Fairchild's reaction, I don't know her well enough to comment. But medically speaking, it is not uncommon for a relative to experience some kind of relief after watching a loved one suffer for so long... All I know for sure is that I went straight home after seeing Mrs. Fairchild to her door last night."

"Do you have an alibi for last night, Dr. Alexander?"

"*I* don't normally make a habit of ensuring alibis when *I* go to sleep at night, *alone* in my bed."

"Don't get smart with us, young man," shouted the plainclothesman. "You may be a big shot at the hospital, or with the ladies, but to us you are nothing more than the man who was with the wife of the murder victim the night he was killed."

The other officer added, "Look, mister, we really don't care who you sleep with, but the trouble you could be getting yourself into right now is far more serious than adultery. If Mrs. Fairchild can vouch for you and you for her, and you can prove that neither of you left this place, you may be saving yourselves a lot of hassle—for now, anyway."

"You've already suspected, tried and convicted me without a hearing, and now you want me to hand you a motive? I think not! I'm innocent, and I intend to prove it."

Having said that, Jake wanted to walk away from the beautiful Mrs. Fairchild and her seedy problems, but couldn't. She looked so alone and terrified. Besides, his curiosity and sense of adventure were getting the better of him, dragging him into it by the collar.

As the plainclothesman interrogated Samantha on the situation in the Far East, Jake realized if he was going to stick around and help her, he had better get her some good legal counsel—*fast.*

"Aren't you supposed to read her her rights to an attorney before forcing information out of her?"

"We're not arresting her—not yet, anyway. But if it will make you feel better, go call a lawyer—it's your quarter."

"Samantha, I absolutely insist you not say another word until I get you an attorney."

"And, Jake, I insist you not get involved."

The sleazy-looking journalist grinned, showing all his nicotine-stained teeth, and sarcastically

said, "Ain't love grand," while snapping a shot of
Jake standing next to Samantha with his hand on
her satin-robed shoulder, comforting her.

Infuriated, Jake nearly ripped the camera out
of the journalist's hand and shouted, "You insensitive creep! The lady just lost her husband! Now
pick up your gear and get the hell out, before I—"

"Call the police?" the journalist mocked as he
walked out with a big smile on his face.

The stout policeman smirked back at him,
and said, "We'll be off, too, for now. But make
no mistake, we will be back, so *don't* get any
ideas about leaving."

After ushering the obnoxious team out the
door, Jake held Samantha in his strong, sinewy
arms, and said, "I'm really sorry about your husband. I still can't imagine who would want to do
something like that... I have a feeling I've walked
into something big. I'd really like to help you
through whatever you have become involved in.
But before I can do that, I need to know *everything. You* must not hold anything back."

Jake was terrified at what he might discover
about his dream-girl. She could be a terrorist, for
all he knew. But deep down he hoped she was involved in a noble cause—for that was the woman
who came to him for help on all those restless nights.

Samantha sobbed into her palms uncontrol-
lably, while Jake anxiously awaited her reply. After a long pause, she finally wiped her eyes and
looked up at him. It was time she start revealing
what little she knew.

Samantha explained that it all had started when
her brother Allen decided to visit his age-old pen
pal, Norman Fairchild. Norman was the sole son of
a missionary couple, who was born and raised in
India. Although his parents had encouraged him

to return to the West when they retired, Norman chose to stay back, relinquishing all rights to citizenship in the West. He had never intended to leave, because India was his country. It was the country he was born in, the country he loved and enjoyed. He identified with the people. He was part and parcel of the culture that was just as unpredictable and extreme as himself. Norman had always felt that the only way to live was by being in a country where anything could, and did, happen. To him, India represented tradition, history, philosophy, tragedy, fantasy and ultimate sensuality.

Norman's lifetime passion was to publish a book that represented a compilation of customs and practices—from the commonplace to the bizarre—of his native country. He had managed to gain enough people's confidence to mingle into every ritual—licit or illicit.

Having completed his first volume a year ago, Norman decided upon a brief hiatus. He convinced Allen to join him in a tour during that time, to experience the beautiful India described endlessly to him through letters. The very customs and exploits that Norman had taken for granted as part of a five-millennia-old unchanging culture got a very different reaction from Allen. Despite the beauty and simplicity of most practices, he was appalled at what young women from poor backgrounds—whose parents couldn't afford a dowry—had to go through. So Allen persuaded Norman to betray their confidence and expose them to the world. Being self-righteous and idealistic, he encouraged him to emphasize every gory detail, exposing the mighty in control of the meek.

Nobody could tolerate a man accusing poor parents of selling their teenage daughters for prostitution, or "upright citizens" hurting young brides to extort more dowry—least of all people who might, in fact, be that cruel. What followed was an enraged reaction from the locals being accused. A dear friend encouraged Norman and Allen to escape immediately to Calcutta, where they could mingle into the crowds and make arrangements to flee the country.

Allen employed the very corrupt ways he had always abhorred to arrange an overnight wedding between Norman and Samantha, in order to get him out quickly. His life depended upon it. Samantha confessed that she did it more for Allen than Norman, since her brother wasn't about to abandon his friend after dragging him into all of that. Besides, he would have perjured himself if she refuted his claims of Norman and herself having an old-fashioned love affair—via letters—all those months.

Samantha described the romantic farce as amusing—in retrospect—from taking the first available flight to Calcutta, concocting love letters on the plane, all the way to Norman's penmanship displaying a "sincere" desire to culminate the romance with marriage.

The phony wedlock settled things, but only momentarily. Returning to Queens, Norman and Allen let down their guard. A few months down the road, they were met with an unusual car crash. It claimed Allen's life, and left Norman disabled.

Following the technical account, Samantha covered her pained expression with her palms and composed herself. After a brief pause, she slipped her hands down to grab her shoulders, with arms crossed over in front—emphasizing her need to be held. She then went on to describe the personal aspects of her relationship with Norman.

The union with Norman had never been anything more than a platonic friendship. As for the in-name-only marriage, it was to be terminated right after he got his citizenship papers. But following the accident, it ended up saddling her with the responsibilities of a wife. His care drained almost all of her life savings, since he didn't have any health insurance. She had no choice. He had no one else who wanted to bother with him. And according to Immigration, she *had* pledged to be liable for him. As of late, she had pretty much come down to her last few hundred dollars, not knowing what would happen next. Samantha admitted that the turn of events must look awful to Jake— with her now having only funeral expenses and legal counsel to worry about. But she assured Jake that the murder had been committed by the same people who were responsible for the car crash. They were finishing off what they had started. She linked their locating her to the photo and the article in the newspaper.

Jake and Samantha stood under the dark canopy of black clouds and rain as the minister performed a brief ceremony to bury Norman Fairchild. The gloomy weather about them seemed to signal impending doom.

Other than the clergy and the two of them, no one appeared to be around, although Jake was certain the police was surreptitiously lurking about somewhere. Jake's heart went out to Norman. It really wasn't his country—he never got to know a soul. No one was present to shed a tear or pay him last respects, no one to mourn or miss him.

Tearfully, Samantha conceded, "Poor Norman. Judging by the turnout, one would never guess that at one time he was actually loved, respected and admired by many. It almost feels like a lifetime ago. I guess he never really got comfortable in this culture. The only friend he made here—if you can even call her that—was some selfish curator who seemed to hang around a lot in his last days. But from what the nurses told me, her presence appeared to upset him more than anything else. Never met the woman myself."

Jake walked Samantha back to his RX-7. As he opened the car door for her, a man in a gray pinstriped suit scurried toward them. His sullen expression matched his nondescript features. Despite the mud that tried to anchor him into the ground, he raced his short legs toward them, making it obvious that he wanted to catch them before they left.

Upon reaching the car, he huffed almost breathlessly, "Are you Mrs. Samantha Fairchild, wife of the deceased Mr. Norman Fairchild?"

Not recognizing the gentleman, Samantha looked quizzically at his expressionless eyes.

"I'm sorry, I should have introduced myself. I'm Robin Hutton, Mr. Fairchild's insurance agent. I have with me a check in the amount of five thousand dollars to cover the funeral expenses. The remaining two hundred and forty-five thousand dollars will be dispensed following the investigation."

"A quarter-of-a-million-dollar life insurance policy for a man who didn't even bother to buy health insurance? Kind of unusual, wouldn't you say, Samantha?" Jake inquired suspiciously. "What I'd like to know is how does an ordinary unestablished writer justify such an amount?"

"Don't make any accusations, Jake. I wasn't even aware he had a policy. None of this makes any sense to me."

The short, pudgy man quickly interrupted. "Mr. Fairchild was adamant about taking care of you, should anything happen to him. His associate made a point of insisting that I draw up the best policy possible."

"Did you say his associate? Mr. Fairchild was a freelance writer, desperately struggling to get by. He didn't have an associate. Did you ever actually meet Mr. Fairchild himself?" Samantha inquired.

"No, ma'am. The associate did all the negotiating, since Mr. Fairchild was too busy."

"I should have known. Someone has worked very hard at planning this thing. Norman couldn't have even afforded such a policy. The little money that he brought with him dwindled to nothing after the exchange. May I please have your card...Mr. Hutton, is it?"

"Yes, of course."

Robin Hutton handed them each a business card and went off on his way, not looking the least bit concerned.

Jake became frightened beyond belief. It wasn't looking very good for his dream-girl—not even to him. She could have planned the whole ordeal to break even with her losses and run, while ridding herself of the burdensome husband she was hard pressed to cry for. But Jake couldn't ignore the fact that Samantha had visited Norman faithfully and talked about him compassionately. In all fairness to her, he realized it was still possible that someone else could have killed Norman Fairchild and arranged everything to make her take the fall. After all, she was the only accessory who had escaped unpunished. Then again, if her story was true, why had the auto crash not been investigated more thoroughly? Who exactly was avoiding a scandal—treating it as an ordinary car accident, with no one to blame?

Once again, Jake seriously considered getting out of the whole damn mess—fast. He decided to give Samantha a good-bye kiss and leave her life forever.

Samantha secured herself with the safety belt in Jake's passenger seat, ready to leave the morbid place where she had recently laid her brother and Norman to rest. She arched down her torso to meet her knees, putting her body in a comforting fetal position. Tears, rain and sweat made her makeup run and smudge across her face, making it look like the painting of a child who had a lot to say but couldn't clearly express it.

Jake looked at her helpless appearance. Her face bore a replica of the expression that had accompanied her outstretched arms many times before, reaching out for his help. Her vulnerability begged his reassurance. Jake couldn't avoid her any longer. He gently kissed her chin as she stared hungrily at his mouth with the smoldering eyes that drew him to her in the first place. Jake moved his mouth up over hers, devouring it passionately, all the while telling himself that she was *real* this time.

"Not here, Jake. I'm in enough trouble already. All I need now is to be seen kissing you right after burying my anonymously insured husband."

"Don't forget, I'm a suspect too. For all they're thinking, I could have done the deed to have you all to myself."

"You have to agree, I would have a lot more to gain than you, Dr. Alexander. Incidentally, why are you helping me?" Samantha asked skeptically. "I find it odd that you appeared quite suddenly in my life, playing a critical role almost overnight."

Jake snapped, "I won't even dignify that one with an answer," while fully appreciating the reasons each had for mistrusting the other. It made for a quiet drive back into town.

Jake finally broke the silence with, "Would you like me to take you back to the townhouse, or would you prefer to come back to my flat—for safety and companionship?"

Having said that, Jake hesitated, wondering how he could possibly trust this woman. He didn't really know her all that well, outside of being caught with her in this predicament.

Watching the uncertainty in his face, Samantha said, "Before I decide anything, I'd like to be reassured that you're not going to spend the evening accusing and cross-examining me. I've already had quite the day."

CHAPTER THREE

The magnetic force that drew Jake and Samantha together was so strong that Jake blocked out his doubts about her. He was just glad that she had chosen to come back to his place.

Samantha tried to make herself comfortable on Jake's masculine-looking, black leather couch. It was juxtaposed against exquisite traditional pieces of furniture, a few very rare artifacts, and sensual lacy curtains.

Looking at her surrounds, she commented, "Interesting. Has the appearance of unduly disparate styles blending."

Jake chose to let the comment go, since it was more a statement than a question. "Shall I order up some Chinese food? You never know when the goons will be back to destroy our appetites. Besides, you haven't eaten much since yesterday."

"Please, go ahead. But don't go overboard on my account. I'm not sure how much I will be able to stomach."

Jake ordered a preselected menu for two. It consisted of hot and sour soup, spring rolls, house fried rice, ribs, sweet and sour chicken and fortune cookies—a basic, average, boring selection that neither excites nor disturbs the palate.

"It's going to take about half an hour. Why don't you shower and change in the meantime?"

"Change into what? Let me guess—you have the perfect little see-through teddy, just waiting for your female guests."

"Not quite. I was just thinking of one of my shirts. But if you want a sexy teddy, I'm sure I can pick one up for you," Jake laughed to lighten her up.

Samantha emerged from the shower looking

radiantly beautiful. Jake's loose T-shirt outlined the magnificent curves in her five-foot-seven-inch frame. Dark hair danced by the sides of her face in natural waves tightened by humidity. Although she had informed Jake that she was thirty-four, her innocent face made her look like she was an inexperienced teenager.

Jake ogled her brazenly, with a poignant interest in her nipples, hardened against the T-shirt. As luck would have it, Samantha was bailed out of the awkward moment by the timely delivery of the take-out meal.

Famished, Jake catered to his prodigious appetite by devouring his share quickly, while Samantha quietly played with hers. Jake observed her little ritual with her chopsticks twirling around the food. As benign as it was, her dexterity excited him. Then again, anything she did would have had the same effect—it was more a matter of her mere presence driving him crazy than the act itself. But despite his expertise with women, Jake avoided his dream-girl. Having a possible murder charge pending was enough to knock anyone off track!

Jake's apartment became increasingly clammy as the humidity from the shower slowly made its way into the living room. Jake noticed Samantha's moist T-shirt clinging to her body like a wet tissue.

Catching his unrelenting stare, she swiftly jumped to her feet. "Your air conditioning doesn't appear to be working. May I open your bedroom window to encourage a cross-breeze?"

"Thanks. That will be nice. The superintendent is an eternal procrastinator when it comes to fixing things. He has a knack for turning a deaf ear to repeated requests for basics. I've been meaning to move to a nicer place, but I'm too used to this convenient location."

Jake prolonged his conversation, so as to have an excuse to follow Samantha into the very room in which his mind had become involved with her. As she opened the window, the shell chimes started their usual dance, getting tangled up in the lace curtains blowing into them. Samantha held her face into the breeze, trying to dry herself. Jake sneaked up right behind her, under the pretense of doing the same.

Samantha informed Jake of her head reeling and the room spinning crazily, then fainted helplessly into his arms. Jake believed it was a response to a combination of heat, fatigue, stress and dehydration. He carried her to his bed and checked her pulse. Feeling reassured, he proceeded to stroke her cheeks, while softly calling out her name in hopes of awakening her. Samantha suddenly came to, with Jake leaning above her in his warm, soft, four-poster bed. She looked at his pelvis—turgid against her thigh—and smiled. She appeared to be both amused and delighted at her effect on him. Jake began pouring a trail of kisses across her long, swanlike neck, traveling right down toward her covered bosom. Samantha's taut nipples and perky breasts defied her—along with the big moan that escaped her—as she unconvincingly protested.

"Are you still afraid of us getting caught in the act?" Jake asked.

"No, I'm just not ready for a relationship."

"Who said anything about a relationship? You yourself have proven that sex and a relationship needn't go hand in hand," Jake laughed.

"That's not funny, Jake."

Since the mood was definitely lost, Jake decided to go into the other room and make an after-dinner liqueur for himself. As he sipped away on the velvety nectar, he broke open one of the fortune cookies. It said, "Danger lies ahead—watch out for mysterious people."

Jake crumpled up the fortune and targeted the waste paper basket with it, grunting, "How appropriate."

Samantha returned, fully dressed in her own clothes. "I'm sorry to have disappointed you... I guess you want me to leave now. I'll call a cab. I don't want to bother you anymore. I feel indebted enough."

Jake felt like a real jerk for having been so insensitive and pushy. He folded his hands together in a prayer-like fashion and begged, "Please forgive me."

Samantha responded by raising her brows questioningly, clearly showing her doubts.

With index and middle fingers gesturing like a salute against his forehead, Jake promised, "I won't try anything again. Scout's honor."

Samantha gave Jake an ambiguous glance and decided to stay. "I'm really tired. Mind if I crash on your couch?"

"As a matter of fact, I do mind, because I'd rather you take the bed," Jake smiled.

Feeling too drained to argue, Samantha accepted and retired to Jake's bedroom, closing the door behind her. As Jake tried to get comfortable on the couch, something hard jabbed his back. It was Samantha's handbag. Jake wondered what a lady's purse could carry that felt that hard. But as tempting as it was, he resisted the urge to examine it, knowing it would be an invasion of her privacy.

Reluctantly, Jake put aside the clutch and tried to go to sleep—but couldn't. A persistent nagging feeling told him to survey its contents. After all, *she* was free to peruse his dwelling, when *he* didn't know anything about her.

To his horror, he found that the hard object was a Beretta handgun—small, but powerful. Jake wondered if it was for self-defense, but quickly dismissed the thought. He had already made too many excuses for Samantha, despite the cards stacking up high against her.

Looking for her hairbrush, Samantha came out of the bedroom to get her purse. As she opened the door, she found Jake going through it. Samantha became furious with him.

"What the hell—!"

"Go ahead, tell me the gun is just for self-defense."

"What gun?" Samantha inquired with a start.

"You're too much, lady. I suppose you are going to say that someone just happened to plant it in your purse—you know, to make it look bad for you."

"I thought you gave me your word on not accusing and cross-examining me tonight. But I guess I was wrong, because obviously you can't seem to let it go."

Samantha grabbed her bag out of Jake's hand—leaving the gun behind—and bolted out of his apartment before he could say another word.

Jake got up and locked his door. On his way back to his bedroom, he kicked his couch and said, "It's just as well she went now before I get in any deeper. I wouldn't have had the guts to send her away myself."

Jake turned off the lights and reclaimed his bed. As he dozed off, he wondered if dreaming about her would still bring him the same thrill it once did.

Samantha Fairchild returned to Jake's dreams. This time not as food for erotica, but as a helpless person changing back and forth between a woman and a child, trying to cope with her crises—much like Alice in Wonderland. Once again, she managed to rob Jake of a good night's sleep.

Jake sprung up in his bed, covered in a cold, anxious sweat. He tried to convince himself that the dream was nothing more than a guilty response to having abandoned her, despite her needs.

In spite of the lateness of the hour, Jake decided to give Samantha Fairchild a call. He thought he should check on her and apologize immediately. His Monday morning schedule wouldn't allow him to touch base until it might be too late to bury the hatchet. Besides, a good night's sleep would be out of the question if he didn't do the decent thing and call—especially in light of her cry for help in his dream.

Not hearing a response at Samantha's end, Jake's heart began to race. The possibilities were endless. She could be avoiding the townhouse for safety. Or, for all he knew, she could have skipped town with her insurance accomplice. Worse, she could be in danger—captured by savages who were not afraid to kill. It was the last possibility that frightened Jake the most-especially since she had nothing to protect herself with, thanks to him.

Jake grabbed his keys and darted out the front door to head over to Samantha's—knowing full well that he was not very likely to find her there.

He could feel his stomach churn and his chest pound as he raced his fiery red RX-7 into the unknown. A downpour started, making the visibility poor. Red taillights reflected off the glistening wet pavement, adding color to the drama of the raindrops on Jake's windshield.

Jake pulled into the driveway of the unlit townhouse. Seeking shelter from the deluge with his hands cupped over his head, he ran to the front steps.

Pounding away at the door, he yelled, "Open up, Samantha! It's Jake! Please forgive me! I'm here to help."

Not getting a response, Jake wondered whether she was just avoiding him, or if she truly wasn't there. He strained his eyes to take a peek through the glass panel next to the main entrance. The place looked completely dark, but just as he was about to turn around, lightning shed a silvery glow and illuminated the inside of Samantha's townhouse. Jake was horrified to see that the place had unquestionably been ransacked. What was worse, a trail of blood led from the living room to the stairs. Without hesitation, he broke the pane with a hanging planter and unlocked the door to let himself in. If there was anyone around, they were bound to have been startled by the crash. Jake wished he had brought the gun with him. Quietly he made his way up Samantha's stairs with cautious and measured steps. Following the heavy trail of blood to her bedroom, he found her lying motionless on her bed.

Jake felt sick to his stomach as he realized he could have prevented her getting hurt, had he trusted her. It was obvious she was not to blame. Somebody had come after her. With bile regurgitating in his throat, Jake probed her neck with his right hand, feeling for a pulse.

"Thank God, you're still alive. I thought I had lost you."

Samantha awakened to find Jake hovering over her in the dark. Her mouth formed a scream, but her vocal cords appeared to be paralyzed with fear.

Jake reassured her and inquired, "What happened?"

Samantha sat up, composed herself and said, "When I returned from your flat, I discovered that someone had broken into my place. I wasn't sure if it was a coincidental robbery or if I was being sent a message. The more I looked around, the more I realized they were looking for something specific... Please don't ask me what, for I haven't a clue."

"Why didn't you call the police, or anyone else for that matter?"

"I didn't feel like facing the police again after such a short while. As for someone else, I didn't want anyone involved. I feel bad enough that you got dragged into it. Besides, if they really want me, I'm sure they'll hunt me down wherever I go."

Jake looked at the pool of blood spreading beside Samantha's leg. "What is all this blood from?"

"I cut myself on a broken vase I didn't see." Samantha interrupted the flow of the conversation by looking at Jake in a perplexed way. "What are you doing here, anyway? And how the hell did you get in?" she asked.

"I phoned earlier to apologize. Hearing no response, I got worried and rushed right over. When you didn't answer the door, I decided to take a peek, to see if everything was all right. Seeing the condition of your living room, I smashed the glass by the front door, and let myself in. Didn't you hear me?"

"No, Jake. I guess I was completely out of it, since I had taken a sleeping pill. I had to. I couldn't cope with what had happened...and the pain in my leg was simply unbearable. I needed to block out everything, to get a good night's sleep."

"Samantha, I'm really ashamed of myself for letting this happen to you. Please forgive me. I will trust you implicitly from now on... And I promise you, together we *will* get to the bottom of this. You will never be safe otherwise. But whatever we do, we need to move promptly. These people are bound to come back."

"I guess we should really call the police. Seeing my place like this certainly can't hurt our case."

As calculating as her statement was, Jake decided to give Samantha the benefit of the doubt. But he knew that the police would not be as generous—they would interpret it as a scam to deliberately mislead them. "I think we need to think hard before we call the police. It could backfire. And at this point, we can't afford anything short of a very cautious approach. Why don't I get my medical bag and tend to your wound. We can talk about it then."

Jake went out to his car and brought back the essentials to disinfect and stitch up Samantha's wound. The gash required eight stitches. As he completed his handiwork, Jake discussed his concerns involving the police. Together, they decided to leave the police out of it for now. The less attention they drew to themselves, the better.

Jake tidied up the townhouse, with the exception of the bloodstains that had crusted into the carpet. An informal inventory by Samantha revealed that nothing was taken. Jake suggested they collect a few of her things and go back to his place for shelter. They wanted to get there quickly, in hopes of salvaging some of the night for a rest they both desperately needed.

Back at his flat, Jake discovered that the door lock had been tampered with. Cautiously, he checked around. Everything appeared to be in order, but the gun was definitely gone. Jake and Sam reassessed their situation. Fearing that a professional detective could be bribed or threatened into disloyalty, they decided to conduct the investigation themselves, taking emergency leaves of absence from their respective jobs.

Monday morning was started off with three phone calls: to Queens' University Hospital, Queens' Board of Education, and Mr. Robin Hutton.

The last of the three calls was the most critical. It revealed that Mr. Norman Fairchild's so-called assistant was an unidentified medium-built man with a dark olive complexion and an Oxford English accent. According to Mr. Hutton, he could have been from either Asia or the Middle East. Having that knowledge, Jake and Samantha talked Mr. Hutton into meeting with them, convincing him of foul play. The insurance company was eager to oblige—anything to get them out of the quarter-million-dollar policy.

Robin Hutton's door was already ajar. That didn't appear to be unusual, since they were expected. Jake and Samantha walked in hurriedly, anxious to get on with their important meeting. They had to begin somewhere. And for now, they were sure this was a good place to start.

As Jake closed the door behind them and they both turned toward Robin Hutton, Samantha let out a loud scream. There lay Robin Hutton, soaking in sticky blood, with a bullet hole in his head and another in his chest—wounds small enough to have come from a Beretta.

Feeling no pulse, Jake knew there wasn't much he could do to help. With nauseating fear, they both ran out, hoping no one had heard her scream. Jake's nerves were jarred. He knew that the killer was close by, since Robin Hutton's body was still warm. Someone was definitely a step ahead of them! Someone knew their every move.

CHAPTER FOUR

Samantha dragged herself down four flights of stairs. Although earlier in the morning she had told Jake about the throbbing pain in her leg—with stitches pulling and stinging—she didn't once complain during their escape. Seeing her struggle, Jake decided to help her by carrying her through the long back corridor. They had to get out of there quickly! It was just a matter of time before Robin Hutton's body would be discovered, and the police would be combing the building for suspects and witnesses. But just as they made their exit from the building, Jake began panicking again.

"Oh my gosh, Samantha, I have to go back in there! I'm certain our name must be in Mr. Hutton's appointment book, right around the time he was killed. Neither our presence nor our absence will work in our favor. The best thing will be for me to erase anything that will put us anywhere near his office. Here, take my keys and get yourself in the car. I hate to leave you alone, but I have no choice. We don't stand a chance of getting out in time, with your leg slowing us down."

Jake raced up the stairs, down the hall, and into Robin Hutton's office. To his surprise, someone had already removed the appointment sheet from his calendar for that day. The killer obviously didn't want them to be suspects. Whoever it was wanted them to panic, flee, and be free for something else.

There was no time to waste on speculation. Since the mission had already been accomplished, Jake fled down the stairs and inconspicuously blended into the buzzing crowds near the revolving doors.

Samantha pulled the RX-7 up to the main entrance to regain lost time. Jake told her to drive them to the State Bank on Berkeley Street. On their way over, he used his cellular to call the bank, requesting the preparation of a large withdrawal—almost completely depleting his liquid assets. As Samantha drove, Jake tried to make sense of everything that had transpired-seemingly in fast motion.

"We have to get out of Queens immediately, Samantha. With each new development I am becoming more and more convinced that this is not just about a nasty article. Whoever is on our trail is looking for something very valuable-something worth killing for. And somehow we are supposed to help find it. I hate to tell you this, but I think your brother and Norman hadn't been entirely honest with you—probably with the intention of protecting you. They must have felt that the less you knew the better. The only thing I can't seem to understand is, why was Norman killed—especially since he might have been the one person who had access to the valuable information?"

Having said that, Jake took a deep breath and went back into a thoughtful trance. Blood rushed through his veins, causing his face to feel warm and flushed. Beads of perspiration trickled from his forehead and made their way down to his jaw. Clearly, he was terrified at the thought of not knowing where to begin. One false move and they could both end up like Robin Hutton!

After a long period of deafening silence, Jake finally spoke again. His words quivered as they made their way around the lump in his throat. "Samantha, since we've struck out with our only clue, all we have left to rely on now is your memory. Think of anything that either Norman or Allen asked you to hold for them, that isn't at your place—because whoever broke in came out clean, despite their thorough search."

"Neither of them ever asked me to hold anything, Jake. As for their belongings, let me think... Norman only came with a handful of clothes and some chronicles. The clothes were obviously not taken, and the journals are in storage along with Allen's letters and documents. Everything is in a trunk at my mother's place."

"Well then, that's where we will start."

"But Jake, I'm not sure I want her involved in any of this. I haven't even told her yet about Norman's murder."

"Samantha, it is a matter of life and death. We have no choice. Where does she live?"

"She lives just outside of Woburn. It's about a three-and-a-half-hour drive from here."

"Do buses go there? I don't want us to be tracked down by my car."

"Yes, of course, Jake. You big-city boys just kill me. Why, they even have a small airport for local flights."

"That's even better, in case we need to fly out—because my every instinct tells me that we might end up as far as India once our quest is on its way. Is your passport in order, Samantha? I'd like to arrange for visas, just in case..."

"As far as I know, it should be valid for at least another year. You weren't planning a longer voyage than that, were you?" Samantha added teasingly.

With a worried look on his face, Jake grabbed his chin with his left hand and replied, "I certainly hope not, Sam. Now, here is what I think we should do. I feel the best option would be for us to get everything in order *before* we leave for your mother's. That way, if we need to go anywhere, we can grab a local flight from Woburn to a major city with an international airport. It will work out to our advantage, making tracing us a little harder."

"That sounds great, Jake. You seem to be pretty good at the cat-and-mouse game."

"Don't get too excited yet. We still have to sneak out on the authorities. They instructed us to not leave Queens, remember?"

"That was nothing more than an intimidating statement. No formal charges have been made yet. We can still run before they come up with them," Samantha reassured him.

The bank had everything ready by the time the little RX-7 sped into its parking lot. Jake picked up the money and darted out, leaving behind nothing but a trail of tire marks and the stench of burnt rubber.

Next, they sped out to the Indian consulate. Jake used his position in society to get speedy results at the visa office. It really helped to have a name that opened doors quickly. But was that name going to pass the true test in saving their lives? Jake thought not.

Having organized the business end of things and picking up Samantha's necessities, the two of them headed for their final stop before Woburn—Jake's flat.

Jake looked at his rapidly ticking Rolex and said, "We have a couple of hours before the bus leaves. We should freshen up and get something to eat. I'll drop you off so you can shower and change while I head out to the deli around the corner to grab us some food. And please, find something more comfortable than that lovely dress of yours."

Having said that, Jake took another glance at the enticing woman who graced his passenger seat.

His groin quivered at the thought of the bonuses that might accompany their exotic trip, where a constant surge of adrenaline flooding their bodies was practically guaranteed.

Jake turned on the shower for Samantha and adjusted the jets in the brass showerhead to shoot out a combination of velvety bubbles that would caress her body and sharp streams that would treat her muscles to an invigorating massage. After ensuring a comfortable temperature, he rushed out to pick up lunch.

Jake hurried back from the deli, not wishing to waste any time. To his surprise, Samantha was still in the shower. The warped bathroom door was opened a crack, as usual. Just this once, Jake was grateful the superintendent had dawdled in fixing it. As naughty as it felt, he couldn't resist the chance to peek through.

The indulgence of the hand-held showerhead proceeded to satiate the cravings of Samantha's carnal desires. The graceful movements of her perfect body could be seen right through the film of condensation on the shower door. The erotic ritual intoxicated Jake. All the yearning that had been lying dormant since their unsettling plight began came gushing back forcefully as he witnessed her titillate the curly wet nest between her long, lanky legs. She was more sensuous in reality than any of the abstract pictures his mind had painted all those weeks.

Jake gave himself a gentle slap on his cheek, reprimanding his salaciousness. Swiftly, he moved away when he heard the shower turn off. His body envied the soft towel which was sure to be rubbing against Samantha's wet and aroused body.

As Jake laid the tuna-melt sandwiches on the

marble bistro table, Samantha came out from the bathroom. Her fresh-smelling body was draped in a terry robe, while her hair was wrapped in a towel turban. Her face was makeup-free—displaying her raw beauty. Jake had to force himself to look away before he lost all sense of self-restraint.

After a long and tedious drive, the bus finally pulled into Woburn, making its way through picture-perfect streets. Mature vintage maples connected over cobblestone walkways, forming a deciduous canopy. Bistros and vendors' booths congested the sidewalks with animated activity. Jake thought about how enjoyable a leisurely stroll would be, under different circumstances, of course. For now, he just wanted to finish his search for leads, followed by a hasty exit.

The reunion between Samantha and her mother was very emotional. It was the first time they had seen each other since Allen's funeral. Announcing Norman's murder didn't help any. Jake truly felt out of place as the two ladies held each other, motionless. He decided to get right down to business—away from the heart-rending scene. Jake requested that he be shown to the notorious trunk while the two of them shared a brief visit. He knew it could be a while before they would have another opportunity—if they would have an opportunity. Samantha showed Jake to a rusty old trunk in the attic. Blowing away the dust, he cautiously opened the top, safe-guarding the fraying hinges. Jake pulled up an old crate to a window, made himself comfortable, and began surveying the contents of the abandoned coffer. It proved to be a treasure chest of clues. Norman's personal journal and letters to and from Allen revealed the unabridged version of his situation. It was bigger than anything Jake had imagined. It certainly shed light on why someone would want Norman Fairchild dead.

As Jake continued searching through the wealth of information he had engrossed himself in, he uncovered what he believed to be the missing piece to the puzzle. It described the importance of a stolen signet ring that was to settle an age-old dispute between two dynasties.

Jake let out a big sigh, wondering whether or not the ring—if found—could buy them their freedom. Realistically, he knew there were no guarantees, since they might still be killed when the sought-after treasure was located and delivered. Jake gathered anything and everything that might lead them to the invaluable signet ring and made his way back to Samantha.

"Time for us to leave, Sam. I have everything that we're going to need. Now we must head out to catch the first available flight to an international airport. We can fly to India from there."

Tears welled in Samantha's mother's eyes as she hugged her only child apprehensively. "Please be careful, Sammy—you're all I have left now."

The flight to India was full of fears and concerns. While Samantha read through the letters, Jake studied Norman's notes and realized they had unlocked Pandora's box. What awaited them was anybody's guess—quite apart from the perils of not being properly vaccinated or briefed on the country. The uncomfortable flight persisted in its penetration through various time zones—magnifying the nauseating trepidation that tormented the couple.

CHAPTER FIVE

Jake peered through his airplane window, moments before touchdown. A jumble of psychedelic specks approached rapidly, like a moving kaleidoscope. Yes, this was India. He could see it humming with colorful activity. Soon he would be immersed in it.

A blast of scorching summer heat greeted Jake and Samantha as they stepped out of the plane at the Indira Gandhi International Airport, New Delhi. It felt like a stifling sauna, laden with humidity and high temperature. Having cleared customs and immigration, the twosome picked up their baggage and made their way out to the taxi stand.

"Now what, Jake?"

"I'm not sure, but for starters, I'm going to find us a five-star hotel. I just hope they will accept cash without too many questions. Credit cards will make tracking us down far too easy."

Jake wiped his sweat-soaked forehead on his sleeve and continued, "Once we are settled in, I'd like to share what I've pieced together with you. We can then move on to some concrete strategy planning."

Jake whistled down a black and yellow, three-wheeler auto rickshaw, puttering and sputtering on a little scooter engine.

"Best five-star hotel."

"Yes, sahib. Me take you to the best. And if sahib want tour or anything, me get it. Sahib rent me for day or whole week, if he like."

The drive through New Delhi was quite an experience. The main road was divided by a garden island throughout its entire length. Flowers in an array of colors were intermingled with dancing fountains, arranged in various patterns. The cabby mumbled in his broken English—something about colorful lights doing nightly shows with the jets. Jake and Samantha noticed that the burst of vibrant hues didn't just end there. It extended to the clothing and jewelry that adorned the native women and children—different in form, style and texture, but consistently brightly colored.

The actual display of means ranged from extreme poverty and destitution to an obscene amount of wealth and grandeur. While the rich areas boasted homes closer to palaces than residential units, the slums showed dilapidated sidewalks, inhabited by children squealing and frolicking amidst heat, dirt and squalor—right beside mutilated beggars. Despite their living conditions, their bony faces displayed generous, toothy smiles.

As the road wound around the belly of India Gate and made its way through repetitive city segments, Jake discerned that the metropolis appeared to be divided into little communities, complete with schools, housing, shopping and workplaces. According to the rickshaw fellow, it was arranged to facilitate travel by foot, bicycle, or any other means of transportation—all sharing the streets with equal rights. Jake found the traffic density and chaos to be mind-boggling.

Being bombarded by the eccentric, Jake thought to himself, so this is the city where the beautiful, enchanting and powerful Princess Shanti Choudhry lives—the woman who holds the key to settling the age-old feud between the last two royal Rajput dynasties. But her time is about to run out—just as soon as her twenty-first birthday, or the recovery of the infamous signet ring.

Jake resented Norman's involvement in such an omnipotent game, since it had indirectly dragged innocent lives into it. But knowing the thrill his own viscera were experiencing, he could certainly understand why. At times, he almost felt envious of what Norman must have experienced—an intimate involvement with Shanti, influencing history, and being married to Samantha. A jolt of excitement made Jake's spine shudder when he compared it to his own banal existence—up until now, that is. Yes—he was definitely going to enjoy the exhilarating ride, however perilous.

The little three-wheeler putt-putted its way into the majestic driveway of the Oberoi Hotel. Flags from at least a hundred different countries garnished its neatly pruned border.

Jake paid the fare and a generous tip, and asked the cabby to return at ten the following morning—for an entire day. The cabby folded his hands together in a prayer-like fashion, and said, "Namaste, sahib. Sunil be back tomorrow."

Sharply dressed bellboys secured Jake's and Samantha's luggage and piled it onto fancy brass trolleys. The duo was then ushered into an opulent marble lobby—dressed like a tropical garden—with waterfalls and flamboyant floral arrangements. Fine Tabriz carpets dressed the walls and floors alike. Jake couldn't fathom the time and labor that must have gone into such precise, intricate detail. While enjoying the Indian splendor, Jake noticed that the hotel managed to be westernized enough for familiarity. It certainly wasn't the pristine India he had hoped to travel one day. Then again, plenty of adventure lay ahead of them, despite their comfortable accommodations.

As Jake arrived at the check-in counter, the receptionist inquired, "Will that be a queen-size bed with a suite, or a king-size bed?"

Right up until that moment, Jake hadn't even

contemplated the rooming situation. The very thought of asking his travel companion made him cringe. Samantha saw his hesitation and bailed him out by suggesting they take the queen suite option, to conserve funds.

Following their speedy check-in and freshening up, Jake knew that he needed to apprise Samantha of everything he had learned.

Ensuring a comfortable position on the couch, Jake presented the extraordinary account of Norman's involvement in the Far East situation.

The tale began with the recent tension that had been plaguing the country, with various groups vying for prominence-the Rajput royalties being a case in point. With the few regal families remaining, cohesion had become a greater priority than competition to keep them from becoming extinct. Dynasties that at one time were constantly engaged in conflict to prove supremacy one over another now tried to establish harmony, using marriage alliances and iron-clad betrothal agreements. Needless to say, they were taken very seriously, with no viable options for nullification. But the late Mr. Norman Fairchild tried to challenge the very core of such an arrangement perhaps the most compelling one at that, because, if unfulfilled, it could create history.

The contract in question was initiated for the unification of the last of two equally powerful pure-bred Rajput dynasties—the Choudhrys and the Ranas—who had always locked horns in proving sovereignty over each other. Their age-long dispute had continually disintegrated the blue-bloods—secondary to mixed marriages with non-royalties because neither was willing to put aside their differences and marry into the only other family in their class. That is, until twenty years ago, when

Princess Shanti Choudhry and Prince Ranjit Rana were born to their respective lineage on the *same* day. It was seen as fate reaching out her hand, to give the ruling-class Rajputs one final chance at self-preservation.

A decree proclaimed that on their twenty-first birthday, Shanti Choudhry and Ranjit Rana were to be married. Grand festivities celebrated the betrothal that was to unite the two progeny. The National Museum of History honored the importance of the occasion by pledging the royal Rajput seal to the bride and groom in the form of a signet ring. It was to culminate the joining of the two royalties into a single imperial realm. The colossal agreement further outlined that if either party was to back out, they would inadvertently give over to the other all rights to dominion—as designated by the signet ring—thereby completely aborting their own status and future claims as royalty. For obvious reasons, nobody remotely suspected that either child would selfishly go against it.

The betrothed couple not even allowed to were see each other until their wedding day. The elders believed that matters of the heart were bound to stand in the way of proper upbringing and education, not to mention compromised standards. They felt that there would be time enough to fall in love after the wedding was a fait *accompli.*

Samantha interrupted the tense story by inquiring as to how Norman's article fit into any of it.

Jake explained that the article had nothing to do with the enraged reactions against Norman or Allen. It was one of several like it that continually dressed the papers—written by various journalists—in the altruistic hopes of using exposure as a weapon to free people from bondage. There were so many of them that they didn't even flinch an eyebrow anymore, least of all motivate murder. Jake concluded that the article was merely a cover-up to keep her innocent to the lethal information.

Jake went on to describe how Norman met Shanti—her name meaning "peace"—while working on his doctorate on Indian studies. Norman's path repeatedly crossed Shanti's, who was trying to familiarize herself with the history of the Rajputs. Norman's fascination with Shanti grew intensely as he discovered that she was brighter than anyone he had ever met but still naive and innocent at heart. She could win any debate and quote history and politics with an unmatched zeal. Yet she remained totally unaware of the sensual power she possessed over any man who laid eyes on her.

Despite the various women who fancied Norman, he fell hopelessly in love with the one forbidden fruit—a woman betrothed to another man. This carried grave implications.

At first he loved her privately, from afar. But then his unrequited love almost became an obsession. He *had* to have the virgin who was being saved for another.

It wasn't long before he became unable to keep it to himself. He made his love known to her. He toyed with the impressionable princess' feelings by trying his best to convince her to leave the barbaric bargain behind—in favor of sailing away to a life of true love and passion with him. Knowing she couldn't really do that to her people, Norman went as far as promising to steal the signet ring for them, exchanging their sovereignty for her hand in marriage—something they themselves had done, in a manner of speaking.

Samantha inquired about what made Shanti the kind of woman who had the power to change the future and make men lose their minds. Jake replied that Norman had characterized her as having the wit of Solomon, the graceful moves of a jaguar, the timidity of a kitten, and the charisma of Cleopatra. Physically, he described her as having long, shiny, brown hair that gave a hazel reflection to her light green eyes—cat's eyes, as they're known in these parts. Norman also talked about her straight and dainty nose with a brilliant diamond shining off it—almost as attractive as the dimple on her chin.

Jake paused to look at the freckle on Sam's nose and the dimple that graced *her* chin. As he gawked at his object of desire, he couldn't help but notice the fear that plagued her eyes. Jake decided to break away from the story to give Samantha a brief distraction.

Holding her chin gently in his hand, he kissed her dimple and smiled. "Sounds kind of like this little gem."

Jake noticed Samantha's face flush. But inasmuch as he wanted to scoop her up in his arms and make love to her right then and there, he didn't dare make the first move—in light of her response to his previous advance. It was up to her to make it happen.

Samantha's full lips started to tremble as she pressed them against Jake's sensual mouth. Feeling her desire, his tongue began tracing them delicately, whetting her appetite. Samantha responded by reaching down to feel his pelvis. Her exciting touch shook his spine as he realized that his unfulfilled dreams were about to transcend into a satiated reality. The thrill of the moment closed his eyes and sent shivers through his body as he let out a big moan, tilting his head backward. The undulating movement through his body pushed his erection harder into her hand.

"Are you sure about this, Sammy?"

Samantha replied by unfastening his shirt buttons and blowing on the perspiration that glistened his erect nipples. She then proceeded to lick his firm, muscular chest. Her tongue traveled along the thin midline of hair leading the way to the generous mat of curls that announced his phallus. Her hands shook as she tried to undo the buttoned fly on his white linen shorts. Their soft texture and loose cut revealed the excited member that rippled within. Samantha's arousal peaked as the fabric fell to the ground, making Jake's vulnerable organ available to her—to do with it as she pleased. Samantha indulged it by consuming it like a melting ice-cream.

Being totally taken by her ravaging lust, Jake untied the little straps that held up her sundress. As her garment also fell to the floor, her soft sumptuous breasts got perky, and her nipples darkened, becoming taut with excitement. Jake took them, one by one, into the moist cavern of his mouth, teasing them with his strong tongue. He remembered the day before, when she brought her body to complete gratification, and hoped he would not fall short of satisfying her with the same intensity.

Jake's muscular arms, with veins throbbing within them, carried Samantha to the firm, queen-size bed. He placed her across its width, her hair dangling off the edge. Every inch of her body was covered in goose-bumps, despite the obvious heat. Jake began devouring her—licking, sucking, kissing everything that came in his path. His mouth finally landed at the bare film of cotton bikini that clung to her seat of throbbing tension. One swift pull and the obstacle was torn off her flesh. There lay the exuberant split fruit, liberally framed by soft, dense coils of hair, displaying its desire to be partaken of.

Jake salaciously indulged the little soldier that stood firm, guarding her gates of paradise. As he felt her tense and vibrate from the excitement of the upcoming rapture, he entered her. Slowly and rhythmically he thrust into her—trying to give her the unhurried pleasure of Tantric sex—alternating focus between the yin and the yang. His staying power amazed her. He had the vigor of youth, which made for hours of enjoyment, but without the initial delirium that ends things too quickly. Jake persisted in satisfying Samantha's hunger until she couldn't hold off anymore. She lifted her hips against his, engulfing him deeper, and allowed them to convulse in a simultaneous climax.

For the next hour, Jake and Samantha lay undisturbed in each other's arms, relishing what they had just experienced, drifting in and out of the inevitable delicious exhaustion.

Samantha finally broke the tranquillity and giggled, "You have got to stop telling me bedtime stories, Dr. Alexander. One never knows what the tension can do."

Jake pulled her closer, wishing to melt their bodies into one, evaporating the gap that could identify them as two. Intoxicating kisses punctuated his loving pillow talk, capturing the tenderness of the moment. But as luck would have it, the venomous intrusion into their otherwise perfect relationship returned to overtake Jake's mind.

Jake stared at Samantha's beautiful eyes that looked up at him in awe, and said, "Shall I complete your story now?"

"I really wish that there was no story at all, but since that's just wishful thinking, we might as well finish with it. We need to move on to figuring a way out of this mess."

Jake continued. "Since Norman was a very bright man, and an obsessed one at that, he convinced Shanti that he would do whatever it took to bring them together. Being a man of his word, driven by a major goal, he somehow managed to steal the signet ring from the museum. It was the only way he knew to get her to betray her ancestors, since the ring would ensure they were not robbed of their royal lineage on her account. Norman had hoped to keep it hidden until after the negotiations had been completed, but, unfortunately for Romeo and Juliet, they didn't even make it that far.

"An informant told Norman to get out fast, knowing that the Choudhrys were after his blood. Allen convinced Norman to take the advice, since Shanti had already disappeared without a trace. Rumor has it that she is still locked up somewhere within the Choudhry mansion... As for the Ranas, they are enraged over the missing ring-ready for war, if need be."

"How did Allen get involved in all of this?"

"The smell of adventure and justice drew Allen from thousands of miles away, under the pretense of helping his best friend and Norman's charming love, Shanti."

"But why did he have to get me mixed up in a selfish one-man feud against an amicable, benign arrangement?"

"Sammy, the taste of living on the edge can make any man's head spin. We do things without thinking, and sometimes screw up—not knowing how to get ourselves out of potentially lethal situations. Allen probably just made a poor judgment call, under intense pressure and acute time restraints. I don't think he himself appreciated the magnitude of the ordeal he had stepped into. To him, it was probably just a silly arranged marriage."

"What happens now?"

"Now, we both take the rest of the day to read Norman's memoirs, to figure out where he might have hidden the omnipotent signet ring. Because I strongly believe *that* is the purpose behind us being scared off, halfway across the globe."

"And if we find it ?"

"We'll worry about that if and when it happens. My hunch is that the only way out would be to get the Ranas and the Choudhrys together and hand over the ring to the police in their presence—absolving both dynasties of culpability. Any other way could backfire and make their animosity worse than ever, with them deflecting blame on each other. I just hope it works. And frees us."

With that statement, Jake walked over to his briefcase and removed bundles of paper-neatly separated by ribbons wrapped around them like gift packaging. He handed half to Samantha and kept half for himself.

Raising the thumb of his right fist, Jake declared, "Here's hoping we get lucky."

CHAPTER SIX

At ten o'clock in the morning, Sunil pulled up into the majestic driveway of the Oberoi—his broken-down rig shooting out smoke clouds. Jake and Sam noticed the bellboys trying to shoo him away, despite his insistence on being expected. Lucky for him, they rescued their unobtrusive ride just in time.

"I'm surprised at your punctuality. Don't you work on 'Indian standard time' around here?"

"When it come to business, sahib, we come on time. No show, no rupees. Where me take you and the memsahib?"

"Is there a place where we could find the address corresponding to an unlisted telephone number—some public records perhaps."

"You want business, pleasure or person?"

"Actually, it is a family we are interested in locating—a very well-known family, I imagine."

"Sunil know everybody important. Who you want, sahib?"

"We are looking for the royal Choudhry family."

"Why you not tell me that before? Everybody know where Choudhry family live. Me take you there now?"

"Yes, please. And if you can keep whatever we talk about a secret, more rupees for you."

The cabby motioned to zip up the toothy smile on his gaunt face, then fired up the little auto—his emaciated dark hands minding the wheel. Sunil seemed to stick only to backlanes and alleys—honking, shouting and gesturing his way through perpetual congestion. He was either in a rush, or taking the long way to impress them. One final turn out of the slum labyrinth, and he was on a perfectly landscaped road leading to private property.

Several acres of gardens embroidered the front of what appeared to be a castle of sorts. One look and the couple was certain they were in the right place. It was obvious the distinguished family had to have prominence, or they wouldn't have been recognized by the National Museum of History.

As the rundown rig barely made its way up the slightly sloped drive, two armed guards moved away from the overbearing gate and started to walk toward them.

With aimed guns, they inquired, "Who are you, and what do you want?"

Samantha calmly answered, "I'm Samantha Alexander, an old friend of Shanti Choudhry's from the university. I haven't seen her in about two years. Since I was passing through New Delhi, I thought it would be nice to introduce my new husband to her."

Jake was both amused and surprised at her choice of a last name, and his supposed relationship to her. The corners of his mouth expanded into a fascinated smile. Perhaps it was that very gesture that saved the day.

The guards pulled away their guns and mumbled something into their walkie-talkies. After about a minute of deliberation, the couple was told that Miss Shanti was not allowed any visitors— *especially not whitefolk.*

"But I beg of you to reconsider! I'm dying to share my news with her," Samantha pleaded. Still no results.

Next, Samantha threw in a flirtatious stare. It worked. The two faces under the khaki uniform berets relaxed into smiles below the dark mustaches. The taller of the two guards thrust out his chest, assumed a robust pose, and proceeded to talk again on his walkie-talkie. This time, he seemed to push for results, flaunting his rank and title at the Choudhry mansion.

"The big memsahib has allowed you a very short visit with Miss Shanti. You will be taken in by me."

Having announced that, he offered his hand to help Sam out of the little auto, while instructing the cabby to wait outside the main gate. "Rickshaw walla, tum yahan rucko."

An in-house vehicle that looked like a golf cart drove them to the mansion, while the cabby took refuge from the scorching sun under a sheltering gulmorh tree. It afforded shade to his parched body—melting away into damp half-moons under his armpits.

The decadence of the Oberoi paled in comparison to the Choudhry estate. Norman was right— the rich had no better playgrounds than the majestic luxuries of India, a true paradise on earth.

Rare miniature drawings characteristic of the Rajput reign adorned the walls of the Choudhry mansion. They had been created several centuries ago, using paintbrushes that consisted of a single squirrel hair.

Their intricacies were complimented by filigreed marble windows, studded with assorted gems—contrasting against a pink and black granite floor. Bejeweled marble lattice railings encased the chandelier-covered central staircase from which Shanti made her entrance. Her steps were graceful, but tremulous with fear. Jake knew that she wouldn't recognize Sam to be her friend, but hoped she would give her the benefit of the doubt. Fortunately, she feigned enthusiasm—possibly thinking that it was her Norman trying to help her escape.

Following an exchange of greetings and pleasantries, Jake and Sam were seated on a divan covered with embroidered cushions, surmounted by beaded peacocks.

As the threesome visited together, Mrs. Choudhry didn't dare leave them alone—not for a single moment. She plunked her heavyset body on the divan, right between the couple. The red matrimonial dot on her forehead glared like an additional attentive eye, while her silver-gray hair coiled into a giant, ear-shaped bun—looking like an aid for better auditory coverage. Jake realized that despite her smooth talk and deceptively gentle manner, Mrs. Choudhry was no fool. She had all the makings of a dynamic, shrewd businesswoman, with extremely sharp senses. Cautious conversation was of the essence.

Building upon what Norman's diary had revealed, Sam concocted a tete-a-tete that appeared to confirm her friendship with Shanti. She used all the little excursions that Shanti and Norman had enjoyed together—when she was supposedly with a girlfriend—to provide validity to her discourse. It was planned to reassure the mother and encourage the daughter—since it reflected incidents only Norman would have known about. The visit lasted longer than planned, due to the hospitality of a high tea. Jake and Sam knew enough to take it as nothing more than polite customary dictate. The leisurely pace was interrupted when Mrs. Choudhry looked at her watch and reluctantly spoke in a strong English accent.

"I don't want to be rude, Mr. and Mrs. Alexander, but you're going to have to leave now." Samantha jumped to her feet and said, "Yes, we mustn't overstay our welcome."

Without further delay, Samantha gave Shanti a good-bye hug and discreetly slipped a note in her *kameez* pocket, while Jake distracted her mother.

The couple took hurried steps out of the mansion and into the house car, aiming for a quick getaway lest they be found out.

As they made their way to their next stop—the university library—their hearts felt heavy for Shanti. They knew by now she would have read the note informing her of her beloved's death. All the dreams that probably had kept her going during the past few months must have come crashing down to a tragic end, with no way out.

On a more selfish note, Jake and Sam hoped that Shanti Choudhry wouldn't refuse her help to the bearers of the bad news. She was their only hope in being able to locate the notorious ring. Norman had to have divulged something to her. She might even have been his accomplice.

With the rising sun, the choking heat was beginning to drain Jake and Sam. They weren't used to such temperatures. Their fatigue was further increased, since their biological clocks hadn't yet adjusted to the jet-lag.

Jake brushed back a tendril of hair that clung to the perspiration on Samantha's forehead. His touch made her neck and upper body shiver. She moved closer to him and nuzzled her face into his strong neck, with his jugular pulsating against her cheek. The smile on her face—coupled with her distant stare—made Jake hope that she was drifting off into the delicious reservoir of her mind, plotting...

Sunil drove his auto-rickshaw into the university parking lot.

Jake gave him some money and said, "We're going to be a while. Why don't you get something to eat and meet us back here in about an hour."

As they walked toward the library, Samantha suggested, "Based on my background, I think *I* should be the one to read up on the history of the

two families and the disappearance of the signet ring."

"And I can round up some detailed maps of places Norman constantly talked about in his journal," added Jake.

Being in the library always gave Samantha a rush. It was her favorite place to relax. History always came alive when she flipped through the musty-smelling, discolored pages. It never failed to amaze her that even the most brilliant of minds was minuscule compared to the bound leaves of knowledge—for they represented an accumulation beyond calculation. Samantha shook her head to free it of the mind-boggling appraisal and got busy with her research. The more she read, the harder she had to restrain herself from getting too wrapped up in the fascinating stories. They titillated her passion for history. But this was not the time to savor them at leisure.

Jake's search was also fruitful. He obtained historic as well as ordinary maps and made copies of all they would need for now. Realizing that Sam would require more time, he moved over to a comfortable couch, planted right below a ceiling fan. The big, dusty blades spun away lazily to comfort the readers seeking refuge beneath them. Their gentle breeze joined the dim dormant library atmosphere, lulling Jake into a snooze. With Samantha engrossed in the annals, he could have been left there for hours had it not been for a squeaky stepladder shrilling by. Jake looked at his watch and vaulted off the couch. He decided to capture Sam for lunch—before he lost her for good to the towering columns she could have lived in.

Watching Jake approach her, Samantha smiled with a pleased glint in her eyes. "You'll never guess how much I've dug up. I think I could even safely say—the plot thickens."

Jake became very curious and perplexed by her statement. He wanted Sam to disclose everything she had learned right away, but instinct told him to wait for a more private place. A paranoid feeling overcame him—making every eye in viewing distance and every ear within earshot suspect.

Jake took Sam by the arm and said, "Shhhh! Let's get out of here first."

As Jake walked Sam out of the library, he was relieved to see Sunil waiting patiently, with his pearly smile contrasting against his chocolate-colored skin.

"Would sahib like to take memsahib to a nice vegetarian lunch? Me drive you to good place."

Lunch sounded great. They needed a break.

"We're in your hands, buddy. Just make sure it's a clean place," Jake instructed.

Sunil took pride in knowing the crowded city so well. He motored through dingy narrow passages called gullies. They were bordered by doors that cloistered airy-balconied courtyards, designed to create private havens.

After a lengthy drive, Jake and Sam finally arrived at an austere restaurant called Kiran. Stackable chairs were cluttered around chipped Formica tables, dressed sparsely by water jugs, metal goblets and paper napkins. A dusty plastic rose arrangement broke the monotony of the countertop. Dishes clattered in the kitchen, allowing a gusting scent of spices to waft through, announcing the savory menu. Despite the disorderliness and the unaesthetic appearance, Kiran food indulged the tastebuds with the most sensual food orgy, combining a plethora of tastes and textures.

Jake was amazed at the spiciness Sammy could tolerate. He was beginning to see that she liked her life colorful, her food piquant and her

physical stimulation strong. The severity amused him, since it reflected her general intense nature. He wondered if she had weathered experiences so extreme that she herself had become extreme in response to them.

Samantha caught Jake's unrelenting stare and smiled, "Hey, big fella, what are you thinking?"

"Oooh, just that you are so different from anyone I've ever known."

"I hope you mean that in a good way. Now hurry up and finish your food. We have a whole royalty waiting to be salvaged," she laughed.

Jake knew that she was only half joking. Her altruistic nature had him convinced that she truly wanted to solve the mystery just as much for the Rajputs as for themselves.

Jake paid the bill and escorted her back to the "putt-putt."

"Sunil, I think we need to go back to the hotel. Please take us there now, and come back for us tomorrow morning at the same time."

As Jake and Samantha returned to their air-conditioned suite, they barely had enough energy to plop flat on their backs right across the queen-sized bed. The heat had seriously taken its toll on them, and they needed to be revived. The cool air in the room revitalized them, breathing soothing life into their sweating bodies.

"Phew! I'm glad that's all done. From now on, we need to limit our escapades to early mornings and late afternoons."

"I think not, Jake. Once you hear what I suspect, you'll want to move on—no matter what the time. It's almost like a good mystery you hate to put down until you get to the bottom of it."

"You have me very curious. Hurry up and tell

me everything, before I become insane with worry, speculation, and some good old-fashioned paranoia."

Samantha propped some cushions against the walnut headboard—dressed with intricate engravings and ivory inlays—and made herself snug in a half-seated position. Jake noticed that she took her time getting comfortable, allowing tension to build through her monumental silence.

Jake fidgeted impatiently, trying to find a restful spot for himself. He finally reclined by her feet, wanting to massage her aching soles while listening to her discovery.

With Jake at her feet, Samantha began reading through some photocopied materials, almost verbatim.

"It appears that the Rana dynasty had an heirloom that graced the family since the early sixteenth century. It was a necklace that supported a rather large falcon, to honor the legend of Umar Shaikh Mirza—who supposedly escaped mortality by turning into a falcon and flying away. The necklace and the pendant were made as a *navaratna*, or a nine-gemmed charm, created by artisans and savants to honor nine renowned Rajput court advisors. It was bejeweled with large rubies, emeralds, turquoise, corals, malachite, pearls, amethyst, sapphires and jasper—reflecting the style of pieces created in 2500 B.C."

"Sounds like a valuable and irreplaceable piece. Don't tell me that Mr. Fairchild tried to steal that also."

Samantha looked up at Jake and said, "I'm not sure. But according to the Rana news records, a rumor went around that was quickly dismissed. Unsubstantiated evidence."

With her glance dropping back to the pages

and her hands flipping through, she continued, "It indicated that thirty-five years ago an illegitimate heir was born to a beautiful servant girl, who was quietly dismissed immediately thereafter. The night she was banished, she stole the heirloom for her child, fearing he would be swindled out of it otherwise, due to his illegitimacy—even though it rightfully belonged to him, as the firstborn son. When the Ranas discovered that the piece was missing, they searched high and low for the girl, convinced of her thievery. Neither the necklace nor the child were ever found. Apparently, the mother left him somewhere for a secret adoption, and committed suicide herself."

Jake wiped the anxious perspiration off his forehead and pleaded with Samantha to continue.

"I know that it's a long shot, but the age of the missing child led me to wonder if it was Norman. What better place to leave your child than with a couple of missionaries?"

"Sammy, that sounds too farfetched even for our story—you know, in light of a population of almost a billion people, with millions being born in any given year."

"I know that, Jake, but there is more... In his letters, Allen always referred to Norman as the falcon."

"Oh my gosh! Could it be? It certainly would explain Norman's vendetta against the Ranas, and his desire to steal the virgin promised to their sole legitimate heir... I wonder, how much of this does Shanti Choudhry know?"

"*Now* do you understand why we need to get back into the Choudhry palace as soon as possible?"

"Every time we turn around, we learn something new, Sammy. Do you think we're sitting on a time bomb that could claim our lives the minute

we discern too much for our own good?"

"I wish I could reassure you, Jake, but somehow that would be nothing more than foolish optimism."

Concern flitted across Jake's eyes as he tried to think of avenues unexplored. Suddenly his face lit up. "What about Norman's missionary parents? Perhaps they could provide us with some leads. Assuming that Norman was the adopted illegitimate heir, wouldn't they be the ones who would know *everything*, including the whereabouts of the falcon heirloom?"

"It's not that simple, Jake. The Fairchilds decided to disown Norman when he declined to return with them in their old age. Their disappointment in his disloyalty was so great that they refused to make amends, even when he finally came to the West and tried his best to reach out. The only way they were going to forgive him was if he could put his adventurous side to rest and move in with them. I guess it was the Indian influence talking, where the oldest son is to assume responsibility for his aging parents."

"And from what I've read about Norman, I am certain he didn't go along with that," Jake interjected.

"No, he didn't, Jake."

"Do you think they're still too bitter to cooperate?"

"I would imagine so—because as of the time of the car accident, they were not prepared to reaccept him. Then again, I suppose if we tell them about his unfortunate and untimely death, they might just come around out of guilt. It's certainly worth a try. We'll just have to word our motives carefully."

"Incidentally, what are our motives with respect to the necklace?" inquired Jake.

"Additional bargaining power...understanding Norman..."

The impossible-to-discern expression returned to Samantha's face. It worried Jake. He wondered if she was suddenly more interested in the treasure than their original quest. They certainly seemed to be getting sidetracked.

Jake began debating whether or not to interrogate her again. After some deliberation, he decided to hold off, since mutual trust was critical to their game of survival. Looking at Jake's transparent expression, Samantha jumped to her feet and began searching through the remaining materials she had copied earlier at the library.

Nonchalantly, Samantha handed Jake a photocopy of the infamous ring. "Here. Take a look at this beauty. Hunting it down needs to take precedence over everything else, for now."

Jake examined the picture very carefully. It was the first tangible proof that such a ring existed, and that it had indeed been stolen.

The Rajput regalia on the face of the ring was supported by a miniature sword looping below, connecting the two sides. *Navaratna* adornment dressed the insignia, while dyed aluminum inlay—referred to as *meena*—decorated the weapon. As fascinated as Jake was by its intricate work, his desire to find it was fueled only by the power it represented. He could practically taste it.

CHAPTER SEVEN

Samantha couldn't wait for seven o'clock in the evening to hit. It would mean nine in the morning at the Fairchilds'. Anything sooner would guarantee a negative response—something she was afraid of getting in either case. Her stomach churned with anxiety as she listened to the first, second, third, fourth and fifth ring on the Fairchild phone. Her heart skipped a beat and started to pound in slow motion when she heard the sixth ring transform into a click, followed by a "Hello."

Samantha barely whispered a "Hello" herself over the bad connection. It felt like she was caught in a nightmare, unable to speak.

Mrs. Fairchild's timid voice repeated another "Hello," followed by, "Is anyone there?"

Samantha took a deep breath to gather enough courage to conduct her very vital conversation. Jake showed his support by standing behind her and rubbing her tense shoulders.

"Mrs. Fairchild, this is Samantha—Norman's wife. I have some very bad news. I don't know quite how to tell you this...but Norman has been murdered."

The blood-curdling scream and sobbing at the Fairchild end made Sam realize that ardent feelings still remained. She was overwhelmed by the emotional pain her news incited. But she had to press on, in spite of it.

Sam continued in a quivering voice, "I know that nothing could possibly comfort you right now, but for what it's worth, I'm trying my best to find who did this and why. I have reason to believe that it all ties in with something that happened in India. As a matter of fact, that is where I am right now."

Mrs. Fairchild finally interrupted, almost incoherently, "You mean to tell me that you buried him without telling us anything?"

"I'm very sorry, ma'am. But I felt it best, since Norman wouldn't have wanted your pity in death if he couldn't have your acceptance in life."

"So what exactly do you want from us now?"

Sam stood face to face with the question she had feared ever since she first decided to call. She had to measure her words carefully—alienation was a risk she could simply not afford. She needed their help.

"I just thought you ought to know...and I hope you will help me get to the bottom of this."

"Young lady, we are hardly in any shape to go on a wild goose chase to satisfy your whims."

"I wouldn't ask that of you. I just need some information that might be critical in helping me solve the mystery. I must do this for Norman's sake, and for my own safety. Please say you'll help me. I'm desperate, with nowhere else to turn."

"I'm sorry, but I can't promise you anything. You've just laid a heavy burden on my shoulders, right after shaking down my very core and foundation. I will need some time to think it over," sobbed Mrs. Fairchild.

"I understand... Please take down my number, and call me back whenever you feel up to it."

Sam recited a series of numbers, uninterrupted. She gathered they were written down, although no such indication had been made.

The elderly Mrs. Fairchild quickly concluded the conversation with, "I can't talk anymore," and hung up the phone without making any commitments.

Jake looked at Sam's strained and disappointed face, and said, "At least she took your number and didn't slam the proverbial door in your face."

"I wish I could be certain of that, Jake."

Jake wrapped his arms securely around Samantha, hoping to reassure her with his support. He wanted to kiss her, squeeze her, make love to her—anything to rid her mind of the predicament she was drowning in.

Samantha nuzzled the side of her face into Jake's chest, with her ear pressed against it—listening to his life throbbing. Her arms reached around his neck almost reflexively as she said, "Have I told you how much I appreciate you, Jake? I don't know how I'll ever be able to repay you."

"Just come out of this alive, and give me a chance at a more conventional courtship. You might even like me. I'm not a bad guy deep down—if I do say so myself."

"I know that, Jake. I just hope we're fortunate enough to have that chance. Nothing appears to be guaranteed anymore."

"Sammy, if this is your way of telling me that you want me right now, I'm game," Jake chuckled, cradling her face in his hands.

Samantha started to kiss Jake's wanting mouth hungrily. Her sensual prowess both impressed and excited him. For the first time in his life, he began questioning if his own expertise could come close to hers. His body ached to invade hers, while his soul wanted her to be his mentor.

Samantha concluded her lingering kiss with, "Hold that thought, I'll be right back."

Jake's gaze followed her right into the oversized marble bathroom. He watched her long slender fingers grab the brass tub faucet, to release a rush of warm water.

As the soothing element filled the tub, Sam returned to him. Slowly she undressed him, arousing each goose bump with individual attention.

Jake stood helplessly and watched her excite him with tender kisses and luscious licks. Her mouth gradually slid down to his engorged organ. One final provocative kiss and she backed away, causing his tormented spirit to pant.

Gracefully she took his hand and led him to the bath. Jake's breathing quickened with the anticipation of not knowing what was coming next.

After ushering him into the bathtub, Samantha poured some jasmine massage oil onto a face towel and began rubbing his back. The more relaxed Jake felt, the harder he battled against sleep—he wanted to consciously savor every maneuver Sammy had to offer. The little towel moved forward to his chest, down to his thighs, and eventually made its way to his aching feet. Jake's eyes closed and his head tilted back as he reclined languorously.

Samantha went to the minibar in their suite and fixed Jake a tall, cool soda. As he quenched his thirst, she slipped out of her own clothes and joined him in the tub.

Next, she enveloped his firm shaft with her soft, bounteous breasts, and vibrated his scrotum with her palms, while her fingers gently caressed his groin. The sensation was so exquisite that Jake feared losing control. He began repositioning himself to lie on top of her and penetrate her pubis—before he would burst into her hands. But instead, Sam gracefully glided onto his manhood and rode him like an untamed beast. With each wild move, her breasts swung provocatively. Jake reached up and captured them, knowing that it would make her convulse fiercely.

Samantha's body responded with unremitting spasms. Feeling her vibrations, Jake thrust into her harder and harder—almost as if he wanted to

impale her. Sam reacted by moving her perfectly contoured hips to absorb his blows into her sensitive cushion, while she resonated with him.

Another series of convulsions followed—very different from the ones before. Moans, groans, gasps and screams left their spent bodies limp, with Sam's torso plastered against Jake's.

As Jake drifted off that night, he delighted in his good fortune in finding Sam. She was a rare treasure with beauty, brains, knowledge, compassion and sensuality. In retrospect, he was pleased with his decision to become a part of her life.

The following morning, Jake tore open the brocade curtains, lined to create complete darkness despite the blinding sunshine outside.

"Wake up, sleepyhead."

Shielding her eyes with her left hand, Samantha replied, "Will someone please turn down the sun a little."

Jake proceeded to tickle Sam incessantly, being adamant about waking her up, one way or another. She finally sat up with a jolt, her body protecting itself in a fetal position, giggling, "STOP."

Then, with a pillow held out like a shield, she said, "I'm glad you're off to an energetic start. I've signed us up for a historical tour."

"Sammy, I hardly think we can spare the time for sightseeing."

"I was hoping it might give us some clues, since Norman seemed to be quite taken by legends and history. Something tells me he hid the ring using his dramatic flare—to be found through a convoluted treasure hunt, designed to buy him and Princess Shanti enough time to escape the country."

Looking at Jake's skeptical, raised eyebrow, Samantha said, "Do you have a better idea?"

"I guess not. I say, let's go for it."

Jake appreciated the fact that Sam's enthusiasm was significantly exaggerated due to her own passion for art and history. Since there were no other plans pending, he couldn't deny her the innocent indulgence. Besides, she might even end up being right—since so far, only the farfetched had made any sense.

Jake and Samantha dressed themselves for a rigorous and adventurous day—him with his light cotton shorts and a polo shirt, and her with a brightly-colored cotton sundress. All research documents and notes came along, to justify the trip. As the couple emerged from the hotel lobby at ten-fifteen, to board the ten-thirty trip, Sunil greeted them with his usual smile and ticking meter. "Sahib late today?"

Jake felt just awful for having completely forgotten about him. A few minutes later and they would have missed him entirely. He apologized for ruining Sunil's day and paid him a handsome wage to make up for it—not that he would have had any trouble hustling alternative rides.

"I come back tomorrow, sahib?"

"I'm not sure yet."

"I come and check anyway. Sahib not worry. Sahib already pay me rupees to take care of it."

Jake nodded, and the cabby putt-putted away.

The mini tour bus finally pulled up into the circular driveway. Its windows were tinted to block out glare. And for those who preferred complete shade, little curtains with colorful tassels had been installed within.

Jake took Sam's hand in his, interlocking their fingers for maximum contact. Sam squeezed hard, eagerly, until her knuckles turned white. The couple climbed up the steps and into the bus.

As they looked around for the most comfort-

able pair of seats and got settled in, a native man changed his own seat. He appeared to plunk himself where he could get a better view of them.

The tour was definitely off to an enchanting start. It began at the famous Red Fort. The dazzling building's grandeur was magnificent, despite the signs of greed that were displayed by empty spaces in the inlays. Precious jewels once rested there, but had since been pried off. A lavish aura boasted the Mogul legacy, as the music of brass bands echoed off the towering walls. Jake and Samantha drowned themselves in the magical sounds, not noticing the pair of eyes that followed their every move.

Nestled near the fort was the Chandni Chauk, with its unmatched warren of little shops selling exquisite, handmade fabrics, jewelry and artifacts. As Sam browsed, Jake stared into the distance, not being one to enjoy shopping himself. Suddenly, his vision caught a glimpse of the man who had made a point of moving close to them when they boarded the bus, and who since then had consistently lingered nearby. Not wishing to startle Sam, Jake tried to ignore him nonchalantly. But mentally, he made a note of his good looks, small frame, and overlapping tooth line resulting from over-crowding.

The trip moved on to India's largest mosque—the Jama Masjid, where pilgrims everywhere muttered prayers. The couple chose to stroll the gardens outside since they didn't wish to offend anyone by not observing appropriate Muslim etiquette in the sanctuary.

The small-framed man also stayed out with them. This time, even Sam noticed his unrelenting ogling. Jake and Sam decided to stare right back at him. Unabashedly, he broke off a lush bunch of hot-pink bougainvillea, and walked boldly toward Sam.

He offered the flowers to her and said, "A beautiful flower for the most radiantly beautiful lady. Go on, take it. It matches your dress."

Jake interpreted the gesture as quick thinking on the part of someone who got caught following them. Looking at the expression on his face, the man put out his hand and presented himself as Feroz Chanan Khan. Following the introductions, Mr. Khan made himself quite comfortable with the couple.

As the tour made a quick stop at the railway station, exhibiting old belching steam engines pulling jam-packed cars, Feroz continued his impressive stories. Their drama was accentuated by the sights and sounds of pistons thrusting to release a pandemonium of ejaculating steam.

The last stop before the old walled city was the world-famous observatory, Jantar Mantar. Built in the early eighteenth century, it allowed astronomers to map out celestial movements. Feroz explained that they used the markings on the stairs within the great bowl as fixed viewing lines under an ever-changing sky. Feroz's general knowledge impressed Jake and Sam. He was definitely a learned man or a scholar of sorts.

On their drive back, Feroz tried to convince them to be his dinner guests. Finding out that his residence was within the city puzzled Jake and Sam. They wondered why a local man would take off a weekday to tour his own city. But since the overbearing man had very much introduced himself into their plans, and didn't seem to accept no for an answer, they reluctantly agreed to go along. After all, if someone really wanted them harmed, they could easily find a way.

Jake and Sam were picked up at their hotel at nine in the evening, in keeping with the local cus-

toms. As darkness took over the amber skies, covering the last shards of fiery rays, a symbolic fear of the darkness started to unsettle Jake's stomach. But it was too late to back out now.

The evening at the lavish Khan estate began with extended family, friends and neighbors, mingling together in the courtyard. It was a beautiful private haven, completely surrounded on all four sides by marble pillars and archways, forming verandahs. Directly above were balconied hallways that led to second-story rooms. A central fountain gushed out sparkling water that could be seen dancing in the breeze from both the tiers. Small island gardens brought further life to the splendid setting.

All present, except Jake and Sam, were well dressed. Gentlemen wore ties and light linen jackets, while the ladies wore colorful *shalwar kameez* ensembles—heavily embroidered, with beads and miniature mirrors sewn in. Bangles jingled on their delicate arms from wrist to bicep, while unwieldy dangling earrings swung down from their earlobes. Elaborate hairdos were adorned with jeweled ornaments and flowers.

As *samosas* (vegetarian patties) and *pakoras* (spinach dumplings) were being passed around, Jake was presented to the male guests and Sam to the females.

Following the introductions, Jake wanted to return to Sam, but she was nowhere to be found. His heart started to race as his inquiries were met with nothing but giggles and foreign whispers.

Jake raised his voice and said, "This is *not* funny. What have you done with her?"

Feroz finally spoke. "It's not what we've done with her that matters; it's what *she's* going to do to *you* that's important."

Jake's initial ambivalence returned with a vengeance. He started doubting her again, wondering if she had been involved with these people all along, and for some reason had lured him as her prey into a tempting silken web.

But before Jake got totally carried away, Samantha returned, looking breathtakingly stunning. She wore a magenta and bright green silk *shalwar kameez*, matching shoes and heavy local jewelry. Her dark hair was pulled up into a ponytail, secured by a pearl clasp, with ringlets trimming her face. Jake couldn't take his eyes off her. As before, he decided, whatever her game, he was going along for the ride. Only this time, Jake knew that there was at least one other person who felt the same way about her.

From the very start, Feroz had not bothered to disguise his fascination with Samantha. And now his blatant stare seemed to be mentally undressing her, envisioning her out of the very garments he had bought her to liven his fantasies.

Intoxicating music of the nineteen-string sarod started to permeate the dwelling. Its notes were slow, sensuous and electrifying. As a small pair of drums called tabla joined in, the intensity of its music became more impassioned, sending shivers up and down the spine.

Jake thought to himself that the five-millennia-old culture certainly seemed to have mastered sensuality in all its forms—treating arousing music, the Kama Sutra and amorous legends as sacred and auspicious. Norman's passion for the culture started to become increasingly clear to him.

Jake feasted his eyes on Samantha. Truly, she seemed to be an invention of this mesmerizing culture—drenched in sensuality. He leaned over and whispered, "Are you sure you weren't created here?"

"*Oh no!* Yet another man seduced by this exotic civilization," Sammy smiled.

Jake's and Sam's private moment was disrupted by the dinner announcement. Being famished at such a late hour was the perfect preparation to enjoy the rich feast that graced the long buffet table. Its delicate aroma tinctured the air, drawing everyone to it.

Mouth-watering rice pilaf, tender lamb korma, succulent tandoori chicken, velvety egg curry and peppery malai koftas titillated the palate with a medley of tastes.

After overindulging themselves, Jake asked Feroz, "How does one ever work off such a meal?" "I thought you'd never ask." Feroz turned to his brother and said, "*Yaar, gane lagauo. Bhangra wangra ho jayan.*"

A deafening upbeat music, heavy on the local drums, started to throb and boom. Jake was taken by surprise, since it was after midnight—on a weeknight at that.

"Won't the neighbors object?"

"That is why it is good manners to invite the neighbors to take part in the festivities."

As everyone, young and old alike, joined in the Punjabi folk dance—Bhangra—Samantha and Jake were also dragged in. Sam insisted on being shown how to do it properly. Jake watched her intently while she tried to master the moves. She had her arms up in the air, undulating to the beat of the music, while her hips swung and gyrated provocatively. With eyes glued to her, Jake's mind wandered to thinking if it was a mating ritual. Knowing the conservative culture, he thought not. But he finally admitted to himself that he had fallen hopelessly in love with Samantha Fairchild—mating ritual or not.

On their drive back to the Oberoi, Jake and Samantha thought over the puzzling events of the day. A businessman with substantial means and acquaintanceship desperately seeking their friendship—totally out of the blue—didn't make any sense whatsoever. One thing was for certain—whatever Mr. Khan had planned, Mr. Khan was going to reveal, in his own good time. For now, they wouldn't dare guess...

CHAPTER EIGHT

Being greeted by Sunil's beaming smile from ear to ear, on a daily basis, was one of the few things Jake and Sam could take for granted. They were especially looking forward to it today, since they had a full day planned, with a major bit of running around to do.

Unfortunately, Mr. Punctuality was nowhere to be seen.

"I thought Sunil was more reliable than this, Sammy. I wonder if someone else bought him out for good yesterday. Too bad. I'd kind of gotten used to him. Let's give him a few more minutes anyway, since he would have waited for us."

Jake and Sam tarried a good twenty minutes before giving up. Their whole day was going to get messed up if they didn't leave without further delay.

"Sorry, Sammy, but I don't think he's coming. Come, let's get someone else."

Jake whistled and waved out to the line-up of taxis waiting their turn for hire. A cabby from the other side of the driveway concluded his break, butted out his cigarette, and screeched over before the next-in-line cabby could make it. The dispute between the two drivers was settled quickly enough with an exchange of angry words and hand gestures. The couple was then graciously propelled into the back seat of the cab that had cut in. Jake gave out his instructions and tried to get comfortable in the lumpy seat, avoiding the slashes across its upholstery.

The little yellow auto flew through the congested traffic, scraping by everything from passengers and bikes to horse-drawn carriages and buses.

Honking was ubiquitous. It was used to tease girls, greet friends, and announce "coming through." Jake and Sam hung on to their seats to keep secure, since traffic rules seemed nonexistent.

The ride finally came to an abrupt stop outside a tall, westernized tower plastered in granite and mirrored glass. It didn't look the least bit like a little missionary establishment the Fairchilds must have started at one time.

Jake fumbled through his money belt to settle the fare. But before he could make the right change, a tall, silver-haired fellow paid off the cabby and opened the door to usher out the couple.

"We've been expecting you," he said.

"I'm sure you have us confused with someone else. We're just looking for an old mission—with no one 'envisioning' our visit," Jake said, sarcastically.

"You *are* Dr. Alexander, are you not?"

Jake hesitated and replied, "So what if I am?"

"Please don't make a scene or push me into using force. Just come along with me. The boss would like to see you."

"Does Mr. Feroz Chanan Khan have anything to do with this?"

"I only answer to my boss."

"Does this boss of yours have a name?"

"Doesn't everybody?"

"Well...?"

"Well what?"

"Well, what is it?"

"Look, Doctor, I don't have all day to play with you. Come with me and you'll find out who it is."

Jake mumbled, "As if I have a choice."

Jake and Sam were raced past a crowded lobby with elevators to an out-of-the-way door marked PRIVATE—AUTHORIZED PERSONNEL ONLY. Their escort unlocked the door and led them into

an elaborate brass elevator, accessible only with a key. Inside the lift were only two buttons. One was marked Ground, the other, Executive Suites.

Jake looked at the man who shared the elevator with them—complete with holster and gun—and wondered if he was facing their executioner. He hoped that Sam had not noticed the weapon. But watching her cup her mouth, seemingly for fear of throwing up, he knew that she had.

Jake put his arm around her shoulder and softly inquired, "Are you okay?"

Sam stood motionless, with a petrified expression across her face.

Judging by the drop in pressure and ears popping, they knew they were flying at high speed to somewhere near the top of the skyscraper. But since no numbers were flashing by, they had no idea where in the building they were. Normally, Jake hated the fascinated stares that elevator occupants give the changing lit numbers. But today, he himself would have liked to see where the hell they were going to end up.

The moment finally arrived. The doors opened onto a plush, red-carpeted hallway, decorated with opulent fixtures and artifacts. It looked more like a garish art gallery than executive suites.

As the double doors were swung open to make Jake and Sam face what fate had in store for them next, their breathing quickened and their chests felt tight. The desk chair that was facing the window, allowing its inhabitant a chance to take in the view of the city, swiveled around slowly with a creak, announcing a heavy occupant.

Jake was completely taken aback to see that it was none other than Mrs. Choudhry. A middle-aged lady, with rolls of fat bursting loose between her blouse and sari, was hardly the picture of the

ruthless beast he expected to find. But depending on what she wanted, she could be much worse. She certainly had the power.

"Please, do not be scared. Do sit down and make yourselves comfortable."

Catching his breath, Jake inquired timidly, "What is this all about?"

Mrs. Choudhry instructed the escort to leave them alone, and cleared her throat.

"My baby, Shanti, fell to pieces following your visit the other day. I pressed her until she told me what had happened. Am I to understand correctly that you two want to find the missing signet ring, and subsequently hand it over to the police, absolving our family of blame?"

Sam replied, "That is what we would like to do—allowing the unification of the two royalties as planned, reestablishing bonds and connections."

"I have given it a lot of thought, and I've decided to help you. Personally. But make no mistake, it is only for my daughter's benefit. If you dare double-cross me, you will experience a wrath greater than the devil's own scorn. No one will be able to protect you then—not anywhere in the galaxy. *Then*, my friends, you can be afraid—*very afraid*."

Jake realized that Mrs. Choudhry used fear and charm to inspire loyalty. Knowing that he would be working with her, he didn't know whether to feel relieved or terrified. He knew where their hearts were, but he was also aware of the swaying power of life-threatening ultimatums from other parties.

Mrs. Choudhry interrupted Jake's thoughts, adding, "Shanti will fully cooperate with you. But no one must ever know—especially not her father. You will meet with her in my office, whenever the need arises."

Sam shifted and shuffled in her seat, crossing

and uncrossing her legs—as if to muster up courage to speak. Her timid voice finally made its way out. "I'm a little confused about something. Knowing your power, why have you not been able to find the ring on your own?"

"We wanted to, but my people haven't been able to locate Mr. Fairchild's private diary."

"We have it right here with us. Why don't we just give it to you in exchange for us being allowed to return safely to Queens?" Sam suggested.

"There are other complications I don't intend to divulge to you. Suffice it to say, you need to find the treasure yourselves, without the Choudhrys being officially mixed up in it. And a word to the wise: be careful with those notes. The Ranas are also after them—and they're not known to be as 'peaceful' as I am."

Apprehensively, Jake inquired, "How do you know you can trust us?"

"My dear son, I'm old enough to know that everyone values their lives, and that of their loved ones. Besides, I had you investigated after your visit the other day, and found out that other than a few distasteful friends here and abroad, you seem to live by the book, *Dr.* Alexander and *Mrs. Fairchild.*"

Jake decided not to pursue it anymore since the woman seemed to know enough, and was holding all the cards. As for her comment about local distasteful friends, he knew that she was referring to Mr. Khan and his clan—they didn't know anybody else. Jake began wondering if Mr. Khan didn't belong to her, or to the Ranas—in which case she wouldn't trust them—who was he?

Sam broke the silence and asked, "Mind telling us what happens now?"

"Now the driver will take you back to your hotel and you will wait for a phone call from the

Fairchilds, in reply to yours... Trust me, it will happen very soon."

"You didn't hurt the elderly missionaries to coax them, did you?"

"No, Samantha. We would never do that. The senior Fairchilds are a very fair people. They always do only that which they know to be right. And trust me, bringing a national cause out of disarray definitely felt right to the old couple... Now, I'm absolutely going to insist that you return to your suite, immediately."

Without further delay, the couple made a quick exit.

As was expected, the phone rang shortly after their return to the hotel suite.

Mrs. Fairchild sobbed as she apologized for what Norman had done to Samantha. She made it clear that she would help in any way possible to free her son's soul of his sinful debts.

Samantha asked, point blank, if Norman was the illegitimate Rana heir.

"You really seem to have done your homework, my child. But how is any of it relevant to your quest for uniting the royalties? Isn't it better to let sleeping dogs lie?"

"Mrs. Fairchild, I have very little to go on in searching for the ring. Any and every bit of information could prove to be valuable. Please, do not hold out on me."

After a long pause that frightened Sam into thinking they had lost their connection, Mrs. Fairchild's tremulous voice returned with a missionary-style allegorical account.

"It was a stormy night. The universe seemed to be angrily crying to mourn the death of our only son—Norman—claimed by a rare form of menin-

gitis. The reverend and myself couldn't understand why the good Lord had taken him away after we had dedicated our lives to serve Him. I held my tiny little angel in my arms, not wishing to let go. The screen door seemed to empathize with me, pounding away at the verandah wall. It continued expressing its rage until it tore off its hinges and crashed down to the floor. I heard a child scream in response to it. I was sure Norman had come back to us, but he just lay there, cold and immobile. The reverend told me he thought the cries were coming from outside. I asked him to go and check it out. Upon his return, he held a little basket with a newborn child in it. I felt it was an answer to my prayers. The infant's body was cold, since he must have been out there for a while. I don't know exactly how long, though. The noise of the storm seemed to have lulled him to sleep— until the door came smashing down. I warmed up his body with a blanket and took him into my arms. He was fair. He could have easily passed for our Norman, so we decided to raise him as such, without ever telling a soul."

Mrs. Fairchild paused. Her painful feelings appeared to be congesting her throat. Sam wanted to tell her that she didn't have to go on, but the ugly fingers of time made her beg the torn soul to continue.

"With the boy was a priceless-looking falcon. I assumed it was a gift from the mother to the child. It seemed to indicate that the mother was a girl from a well-off family, who had allowed her youthful urges to get the better of her, and was now secretly moving on to a new life. It wasn't until the next morning that we discovered the falcon heirloom belonging to the Ranas had gone missing. We were too frightened to say anything, so we buried it

in the church foundation being poured that day.

"As Norman got older, he started to ask questions about why he was so different from either one of us. We couldn't keep the truth from our own son, so we told him what we knew. Norman was enraged at us for having kept it from him all those years. He pulled out chronicles from the library and pieced together who he was. Bitter envy of his legitimate brother and the desire to avenge his biological mother's suicide made Norman obsessed with the regal family. He wanted to rob them of the very pride that led them to treat her so unjustly. When he met Shanti Choudhry, he knew exactly how. But he hadn't counted on truly falling in love with her. When that happened, he became absolutely insane—fighting against forces significantly larger than himself, constantly walking the tightrope between madness and sanity.

"He actually believed he could steal the Rajput signet ring and carry out his plans...but once the powerful jewel went missing, everything blew up. Both dynasties started to accuse each other, ready to start a war to protect their honor. Shanti disappeared and Norman was told to run and lie low, preferably in another continent. That is when he fled, with the help of yourself and your brother. I don't think he was entirely honest even with Allen—at least not until after he was already too deep into it.

"We were extremely upset with how he had conducted himself. Unfortunately, by then our relationship had disintegrated beyond repair. We let mutual hurts stop communication altogether."

"Mrs. Fairchild, do you have any idea where the ring or the falcon might be?"

"The falcon was buried under the north pillar of our church, right by the main steps. Before leaving India, we told Norman about it. I'm not sure if

he dug it up or left it there for safekeeping. As for the signet ring, I have no idea. My guess would be that he hid it some place where one would have to risk life and limb to find it—or perhaps a location that would teach the Ranas a humiliating lesson."

Realizing that the poor lady couldn't offer much more at this stage, Samantha decided to give her a break. "I know this must be very difficult for you, Mrs. Fairchild. But you have been most helpful. May I call you again, if I need your help?"

"Certainly, Samantha. And please take some advice—think from your head, not your heart. India seduces you into thinking from the heart. It can be very beautiful—unless you have a mission you need to be logical about."

Samantha ached for the woman who had mourned her child twice, but still managed to show her love without any bitterness. She wept for her as she relayed the sad story to Jake. Both of them were beginning to understand Norman better. He wasn't the selfish, lascivious soul they had initially thought. In Mrs. Fairchild's words, he was just guilty of thinking passionately from the heart—just like his ancestors of over five thousand years.

CHAPTER NINE

Night fell. Darkness engulfed every form into its black blanket. The moon was no more than a thin, crescent-shaped segment, taking refuge behind angry rain clouds. Nothing but a bare film of dim light filtered through.

Jake and Sam cautiously walked up the church steps, looking at the majestic north pillar that sheltered the key to unlock their mystery. It was critical they not be seen, since they were about to deface a sacred edifice, much to their chagrin.

The couple came prepared to violate a solid slab of concrete hardened by thirty-five years of scorching heat, monsoon rains and gales of winter winds. To their surprise, the structure had already been raped, with nothing but a thin skin of mortar covering its scars. Chipping it away would be a cinch.

The frightened duo would have completed their deed unnoticed by a single being if it wasn't for the pair of eyes that looked down disapprovingly from the top of the steeple. Expert night vision enabled the perfect commander to awaken an army of sleeping pigeons. Their master—an enraged owl—hooted his instructions, ordering the birds to circle above the maimed structure. Flapping wings and howling cries created a riot that was sure to draw attention. Hastily, Jake removed the note that lay in a falcon-shaped empty space, confirming the existence of its prior resident.

"Hurry up, Sammy! We can't risk getting caught by the night watchman. Sitting in a prison cell for months, awaiting trial, will make our mission impossible."

"What about replastering the damaged surface?"

"We haven't the time. It's too risky." Hearing a dog bark in the distance, the couple fled—grateful for the darkness that enveloped them. The race from the scene of the crime continued for a few additional blocks.

A tall wall topped with barbed wire was all that stood between them and the main road, where a taxi could be hired without much suspicion. Jake helped Sam up the six-foot structure. Subsequently, he pulled himself up, and the two jumped to safety.

With hearts pounding within their ribcages, like birds wanting to be set free, Jake and Sam restrained themselves from opening up the note until they were secure in their hotel suite.

Samantha barely steadied herself at the edge of her seat as Jake unveiled the memo. It read:

> *If you made it this far, it's because*
> *I wanted you to.*
> Bravo! For here comes your next
> clue:
> The jungles of Chandnipore hold
> a sanctuary for lovers
> Banished by embarrassed offi-
> cials who'd rather keep it under
> covers.
> Find the maiden who is as fair
> as your princess,
> And you'll be led to a truth that's
> indisputably priceless.

It was obvious that the message was designed to lead someone to a discovery—through a convoluted and time-consuming treasure hunt. Unfortunately, the searching adventurers neither had the time nor the desire to learn what Norman meant by "priceless." All they wanted was to find

the missing jewels and put an end to the political struggle that held them all in captivity.

Jake and Sam became despondent as they realized they had no choice but to play Norman's game.

"Chandnipore, here we come," were the last labored words that came out of their mouths that night.

Finding their way to the little town was a major ordeal, but it was nothing compared to the actual search once they got there. The love sanctuary that the note described was outside the municipality. The only way to access it was by walking through jungles and fields known for their poisonous snakes and scorpions.

Although the site was adorned with four-thousand-year-old sensuous sculptures that could have graced the finest of museums, the entire area had been deliberately neglected—being equated with licentious pornography. The *maharajahs* and *nawabs* who had the beautiful art created to honor the very essence of life enjoyed it in secluded havens, for their personal pleasure only.

Jake was amazed by the magnificence of the sculptures. Some reclined temptingly in tall dried grass, boasting every last detail that had been carved into them. Others displayed completely intertwined couples in flagranté delicto, with amorous stares telling their age-old stories. Still others flaunted forbidden lechery, admiring a budding maiden.

Jake wondered about the people who must have perfected love and passion fashioning the legendary monuments that lay before him. Cautiously, he started to look at the immortal faces of the outstanding mistresses, trying to find one that resembled the face that had been etched into his

own memory—Princess Shanti's.

Angry cries from a tribe of territorial albino monkeys who had taken possession of the impassioned dwelling deafened the unsuspecting couple. Their screeching sounds scraped their spines like nails on a chalkboard. They seemed to echo off the very icons they were guarding. Their virtually human stares and sneers made them look like reincarnated souls outraged by the unwelcome intrusion. The frightened couple barely escaped what could have been a lethal attack.

As Jake and Sam darted away from the monkeys, Sam's forehead crisscrossed with worry and puzzlement. "I wonder how Norman managed to survive them long enough to carry out his objective—unless he somehow befriended them."

Jake sarcastically replied, "Perhaps they permitted him and Shanti the pleasure of savoring the seclusion and ambiance—since their eros paid homage to the stone figures."

The race through the fields was further challenged as clouds that had sheltered the moon the night before started their downpour. Thunder and lightning joined the erupting nimbuses, scolding the intruders' senses. It was as if they were caught in the middle of conflicting elements—being whipped by them.

The duo were drenched to the bone, until they discovered a dense peepul tree that completely shielded the ground below it. They took refuge under its impenetrable foliage. It represented strength, with its ten-foot-wide trunk and thick aerial roots that hung down like ropes. Perfectly preserved leaf skeletons totally shrouded the ground below its protective canopy. Sam picked one off the ground and told Jake that locals used them as little canvases for creating colorful paintings.

Jake wrapped his arms around Sammy. He couldn't help but notice that their bodies were separated only by a bare film of wet, clinging clothing. Her inviting form mimicked the lifelike structures in the abandoned love sanctuary. Jake stared at her relentlessly. Soon, desire replaced the worry that occupied the pockets of his mind. He wanted to make love to her in the surrounding wheat fields, with their yellow stalks swaying to the wind like rippling waves.

The monsoon shower finally stopped, allowing the twosome to walk back while planning out their next move. But Sam's mind was distracted by flashes of the sensual images she had seen that day. She pictured herself lying amidst the inspiring statues, becoming a part of their immortality.

On their return voyage, aboard a bus on a dusty dirt road, Sam witnessed an old stone mill grind away at wheat grain. Its heavy circular moves reminded her of erotic enmeshing, making her pelvis twitch for Jake. She was stunned at how her mind had been transformed by a mere visualization of stone images.

Right there and then, Sammy knew that she had to return to the field of lust at least one more time. She was beginning to see how Norman might have developed strong convictions that eventually drove him to his death. Perhaps that was the priceless lesson he was alluding to.

Back at the hotel, Jake plunked himself onto the couch, coiled up like a helpless-looking shrimp, and mouthed, "I give up."

Sam, on the other hand, started to search frantically through Norman's memoirs. "I know it's in here—something about 'taming the wild beasts with mother nature's own milk.'"

With considerable relief, she held up the paper like it was a prescription for a cure-all balm.

"I have it, Jake! We're going back tomorrow."

Jake had learned to take everything Sammy said seriously. Unquestionably, it was *her* wit and optimism that had made it possible for them to continue their search thus far, without giving in to dead-ends.

"What is it, Sammy?"

"It's right here, staring at us in the face! I remembered that while skimming through Norman's notes I had come across something about how he had turned a wild species into docile creatures. At the time, I dismissed it as irrelevant. But seeing that it is anything but, I've hunted it down. Allow me to tell you about it."

"You have my undivided attention, Sammy."

"In a nutshell, he drugged them until they became comfortable with his non-threatening presence."

Newfound hope peeled back Jake's eyelids, exposing the full circle of his iris, as he inquired, "How?" Following a seemingly deliberate pause, Sam continued. "As you may have already noticed, cannabis—known locally as *ganja*—seems to grow wild everywhere. According to Norman, boiling the entire plant disintegrates it into a substance that looks and tastes like milk. The nectar is referred to as *bhang*. It is the most potent of intoxicants, with some aphrodisiac properties as a bonus. Norman mastered the wild beasts by preparing the compound and serving it to the sentinels that guarded the powerful erotica."

The second trip to Chandnipore was planned out more methodically. The couple purchased a kerosene stove and an earthenware pot to prepare the triumphant ale. Raw materials were not a con-

cern, since they grew in profusion near their enchanting destination.

The bus dropped off Jake, Sam and their gear just outside a scooter rental. They noticed the little machines and decided to lease them, seeing that they were perfect for weathering the treacherous path, not to mention a fast getaway. Barely mounted, the couple began racing them swiftly, leaving behind a trail of dust clouds.

Upon reaching their destination, they immediately busied themselves with the preparation of the formidable brew. Emerging vapors worked to make them a little giddy, and soon they were singing off-key nursery rhymes.

"Can you imagine what drinking this stuff could do, Sammy?"

"I'm counting on its virulent potency, Jake."

Ensuring a tepid temperature, they placed the soul-nourishing milk in front of the vicious legion slowly and cautiously. The monkeys lapped their tongues at it like hungry kittens at a saucer of cream. Once inebriated, they started to move in ritualistic ways. Mating and debauchery were inevitable.

Jake was amazed at the totem pole of authority that was in effect. Having tasted the addictive substance, the chief gave a knowing smile—as if he recognized it from before. Following his cue, all the other monkeys started to warm up to the twosome—confirming an honorary club membership.

"So this is how Norman Fairchild did it! We should hurry up and locate our next clue before they come back to their senses and decide to attack us again."

Samantha looked at the festivities that were rapidly turning into stupor and slumber and said, "I don't think we need to worry about that too much."

Judiciously, Jake began examining the contours of the unaged faces, hoping to unearth one that resembled Princess Shanti's. Unfortunately, he couldn't find any that bore even the slightest resemblance. Samantha concurred.

The sun raced its fiery chariot across the sky, rising to its highest peak. The day languished beneath its terrible white glare. Intense heat started a fierce war against the unprepared couple. Total exhaustion and dehydration were further aggravated by optical illusions. Rising heat shimmered like a mirage, bringing the inanimate structures to life—engaged in explicit movements. Their force was enough to arouse anyone into lustful submission.

Jake laid Samantha down in the tall dried grass and began kissing her parched body. His mouth traveled down to the erogenous zone at the apex of her thighs, and became focused on her hedonism. He wanted to revel in sensations so exquisite that she would lose herself in the exultation of pleasure, stopping time. His touch was almost mystical, subordinating her body to her soul. Jake wanted to preserve the place in his memory by becoming a part of the wonderful things that must have transpired there.

Jake's brutal masculinity finally conquered her, making every fiber in her body flutter jubilantly with tormenting pleasure.

But then...a rustle in the grass ceased their moans and froze their blood—for there lay a serpent, coercing them to continue their search. His piercing gaze projected poisonously out of his hissing, erect head.

The frightened couple sat up with a start, disengaging from all personal pleasure. The snake changed its direction, returning them to their vital task.

A major realization hit Samantha. "Jake, everything in this setting seems to be metaphorical. Why should Norman's clue be any different? The maiden has to be as fair as the princess in her ways, not her looks."

"Wake up, Sammy. These are inanimate sculptures. What ways could we possibly search for in them? If only they could talk."

"I hate to disappoint you, Jake, but I think I'm right. I guess Chandnipore must have our patronage at least one more time. But before our return, we need to find out what impressed Norman the most about Shanti."

"And how do you propose we do that?"

"At the very least, we must reread Norman's descriptions of Shanti."

"And at the most?"

"At the most, we will have to interview her."

"I was afraid you were going to come up with something like that. I guess it's time we say *namaste* to the monkeys and move on."

As the scooters started their return voyage out of the fields, against the blinding orange sun, Sammy screeched to a dead halt, covering Jake in a spray of smoke, sand and grime.

"I have it, Jake! Norman repeatedly talked about Shanti's innocence in not realizing her sensual powers. It seems to go along perfectly with the sculpture of the beautiful pubescent girl who stands alone, bashfully observing the passion, while the eyes of all neighboring males gaze at her with lust. That has to be the one!"

"It may be so, but if we don't leave soon, we'll miss our bus. We'll just have to come back tomorrow, Sammy."

"You can return tomorrow if you like, but I'm going back right now."

Jake grunted to himself, "Strong-willed, motivated and impatient—what a deadly combination."

Going back was one thing, lifting the heavy monument that had rested comfortably for thousands of years was another. It was almost dark by the time they finally moved it enough to check underneath. Jake reached his hand to remove the little pouch buried below it, nestled into a bunch of jostling bugs and worms that had taken residence there. Carefully, Jake brushed off the dirt, trying to avoid any poisonous surprises that might be hiding within.

"For your sake, Sammy, I do hope this is what we are looking for—because today's expedition stops now, before it gets any darker." Once again, the scooters started to make their way out of the fields, hopelessly racing against time and dusk.

CHAPTER TEN

Jake spoke frantically into the phone, "We desperately need your help, Feroz! We're in Chandnipore and we've missed the last bus out. There aren't any taxis that want to drive as far as New Delhi. And to make matters worse, there seems to be no place where we can spend the night. We don't know anybody else. You have to help us, my friend. I'll pay you back."

Feroz reassured Jake, promising him a quick rescue. The wait for Feroz would have appeared endless, if it weren't for Ashok, the scooter rental fellow, making Jake and Sam comfortable. He invited them to join him for dinner in his humble abode, located right behind the shop.

Ashok's home was a small, neatly kept room. It was accessed by a miniature outer verandah, dimly lit by a once-white globe. Being the only light in the area, it lured bugs in the vicinity, frying them to a crisp. Their crunchy carcasses slid down into the heap at the bottom of the sphere, changing its color to gray. The light that penetrated through was scarcely enough to keep one from tripping on the step by the door leading to the modest dwelling.

Ashok seated Jake and Sam at a meager dinette, right near the front door. It consisted of a petite plywood table and four folding chairs. Next to it was a small counter complete with tap, sink and kerosene stove, with a minuscule refrigerator tucked underneath. A small roped cot called a *charpayee* hugged one of the side walls. Beside it was a prayer shelf, boasting marigold garlanded idols, incense, and pictures of Hindu gods. A makeshift casement curtain cordoned off the rear of the room, to provide some privacy for Ashok's aging

mother. The bathroom was located in another area altogether, somewhere out of sight.

Despite the humility of his means, Ashok was proud of his home. His dark, pockmarked face extended a warm smile to his guests as he waited on them hand and foot. Jake was beginning to realize that a warm display of hospitality—even to total strangers—was more a rule than an exception in this mysterious country.

As they finished a meal of rice, lentils, curried chicken, eggplant *bhugia* and hot *chappatis* with *ghee*, Jake took one final gulp of ice water and rubbed his belly.

"Aaaah! Ashok, is there any way I can repay you for bringing our thirsty and hungry bodies back to life again?"

Ashok found the comment to be offensive, and replied in a heavy accent, "You insult me, my friend. You are my guest."

"I'm sorry, I didn't mean to hurt your feelings. But since you hardly know us, I thought we might have imposed."

"In India we believe that a stranger is just a friend we haven't met. And now that we have met, you are my friend, not an imposition."

Sammy smiled and said, "Why do your people believe in doing good to others, even at their own expense?"

Ashok proudly replied, "We feel that showing kindness in this life saves up good karma for our next life—like making a deposit into your future."

Jake could not fathom the unconventional way of life he was being exposed to, as much as it drew him. He felt embarrassed that up until now, his idea of different was a paper parasol in a tall drink, in some exotic climate.

As the couple continued their wait for Feroz,

Ashok served them tea with *gulab jamuns*—sticky sweet balls flaunting glistening syrupy calories, speckled with a shredded coconut coating.

A loud rumble nearly deafened the hushed and almost invisible town. It was Mr. Feroz Khan, peering through darkness and clouds, come to free the stranded duo. Jake and Samantha bid farewell to Ashok, their new friend and gracious host, and climbed into the helicopter of their other novel comrade.

The big blades of the old machine started to spin around like a twirling firecracker gone mad, piercing right through the dark skies of the quiet village. As it began its ascent, Feroz drew out his right index finger and shook it scoldingly at Jake.

"How could you have your woman accompany you to such a dangerous setting? Have you no respect for her fragile form? She was created to grace the world with her beauty, to honor a lucky man with her charm, warmth, wisdom and company, and to bear children. But here you are, dragging her to some filthy hunting grounds. How—"

Samantha appreciated the concern, but was enraged at being treated like a dormant species. She raised her voice and interrupted. "Let me make a couple of things very clear to you, Mr. Khan. For starters, I'm not a spineless woman whose fate gets decided by a man! It was my idea both times—to go there and to stay late. Secondly, I am not 'Jake's woman,' as you put it."

Normally, Feroz would not have tolerated such insolence from a woman, but the latter part of her statement made his face beam with excitement—forgetting everything but the fact that her marital status made her fair game.

"My dear friends. I don't think you appreciate the jeopardy you put your lives in today. There

are wild, man-eating beasts and vermin out there, not to mention robbers and other evil creatures. Please take my advice and avoid places like that in the future."

Hesitantly, Jake said, "You don't understand—we're on a mission together. It's not just a crazy adventure."

"Very well, then. My men and I will help you, but I absolutely insist that Missy be left behind in safety. She can stay at my house, with my mother and sisters."

"I simply won't go for that, Feroz," Samantha said adamantly.

Feroz held up the little pouch they had hunted down but not yet inspected, and said, "Then you can kiss this little sack good-bye."

There was no question that he was serious, because he proceeded to open the window in preparation for tossing it out.

Jake lunged for it, yelling, "How the hell did you get that? I demand you return it to me immediately."

"From where I sit, you are in no position to demand anything. If you care at all for the lady you don't deserve, go with me on this one."

"It's not anything you can enjoy a cut of."

"Is that why you think I'm doing this? You humiliate me. My sole interest in helping you is to protect Samantha. I let her get away once, but I'm not about to repeat my mistake."

Jake's eyes burned with rage and contempt as he wondered about Sam's secret past involvement with Feroz. Suddenly, their "new" friend's undying loyalty was beginning to make sense to him. Jake began wondering why Samantha had treated Mr. Khan like a total stranger. Thoughts raced in his mind—assuming the worst—distracting him from Sammy's surprised interrogation of Feroz.

Samantha pleaded incessantly that she was being confused with someone else. Both Jake and Feroz chose to ignore her.

"So what will it be, Jake?" inquired the smug Mr. Khan, swinging the little bag dangerously close to the window.

Jake didn't know quite how to answer. If Sammy was lying and using him, he might as well have the pouch tossed—right out of his life. But if there was any chance that this was another one of those "mix-ups," they needed the pouch—before the jungles claimed it for eternity.

With cold menace and uncertainty in his voice, Jake finally replied, "I'll go along with you. For now. But Sam and I need to resolve a few things before she takes refuge in your home."

Feroz nobly handed back the little bag, saying, "If this is what you value more than your lives, take better care of it next time. You dropped it out of your pants pocket back at the scooter stand. Luckily I saw it fall out, or I would have never given a second glance to such a filthy-looking piece of junk."

Jake grabbed the sack with a sigh of relief and tucked it in his shirt pocket—for all to see.

The underutilized hotel suite faithfully awaited Jake and Sam's return. Its door was unlocked, opened and closed again, with nothing but muffled footsteps breaking the silence.

Jake turned the pouch upside down over the table and proceeded to shake it, to empty out its contents. A mud-covered broken piece of jewelry fell out. The brilliance that shone right through the camouflaging squalor clearly indicated that it was a glittering piece of art. Jake continued jiggling the little bag until a note dropped out.

As his hand reached to grab the paper, Sam's

hand pounced at it, striking the small scorpion which had attached itself to it. Samantha sustained the sting that was meant for Jake—for he was the one who had disturbed the arachnid's rest.

Samantha's selfless and possibly life-threatening gesture to save Jake moved him deeply. All doubts of disloyalty vanished.

Jake killed the beast with his shoe, then sucked out the toxin from the bite. A local doctor was called. This was out of Jake's area of expertise.

Samantha's wound throbbed and her pain worsened rapidly. She feared her hours were numbered. But time stood excruciatingly still during her wait for the doctor.

The physician finally arrived and examined both the bite and the venomous creature lying lifelessly on the floor. He was relieved to inform Samantha that she was lucky, since the particular strain that stung her was not poisonous enough to claim her life. But regardless, she could be certain of running a fever, requiring constant care for the next three to four days.

Jake hugged Samantha lovingly and pledged to take care of her until she was well again—and always.

"You bravely risked your life for me, Sammy. How do I ever pay you back?"

"Stop doubting me and start trusting me, Jake."

Jake kissed Samantha on the forehead and said, "I don't know what I would have done if I had lost you."

"You're not turning mushy on me, are you, Dr. Alexander? I might just get used to it. But for now, we have to read our second clue."

Jake blew the dust off the note and tried to read the illegible scribbles. He could barely make it out:

Now comes the time to test out
your mind's ability,
Let the games begin, to seek out
your cerebral virility.
The piece of jewelry in your hand
is half of a falcon;
Find its match, and to the next
clue you'll be welcomed.

Sam was distraught at Norman's sick sense of making the clues progressively harder. But as before, she knew they had no choice but to play along.

"Jake, since time seems to be working against us, I suggest you take Feroz up on his offer. I'll only be a liability to you at this point. Just promise me that you will remember—my mind and heart will be working with you constantly."

Arrangements were made and Samantha was shipped away to the Khan estate at the crack of dawn. She encouraged Jake to feign an archaeological expedition to avoid unnecessary questions and doctored answers.

Feroz stood by his word and organized a team that he felt would be most useful to Jake. He excused himself, however, since he had some important things to take care of.

While Jake battled outdoor heat and exhaustion, Samantha lay shivering in an ornate guest bed, with the Khan handmaiden putting cold compresses on her forehead. Her temperature rose, as did the steam from her feverish body. A midday power failure seized the air conditioning and made the situation worse. Samantha became delirious.

Being the head of the household, Feroz was called in. Every measure was taken to save Samantha's tenuous hold on life. Feroz constantly

sat by her bedside, holding her hand, while Jake continued on his treacherous mission.

Following two days of incoherent unconsciousness, Samantha finally opened her red eyes, late in the evening. Feroz became overjoyed, tears rolling down his smiling cheeks. Facing east, his arms shot up, while his mouth repeatedly shouted, "Thank Allah."

"I willed you to live, Samantha, because I promised you I would never let you go again."

"What are you talking about, my good friend?"

Following a long pause and a deep sigh, Feroz began the revelation that put his outlandish devotion into place.

"When I was about eighteen years of age, I met a vision of loveliness called Anita. She looked like you, walked and talked like you, and was smart and strong-willed like you. But most important of all, she had a heart of gold—always honest and loving, never malicious. Needless to say, I fell hopelessly in love with her. I was overjoyed when she reciprocated my feelings—loving me with everything she had. All she ever asked of me was to share my life by getting married. But fool that I was, I rejected her, since she was from a different religion and class. My family would never have accepted her. Eventually, her parents arranged for her to marry someone else, far away from me. At the time, I was certain I too would move on to share my life with a more suitable partner and ultimately forget about her. That was twenty years ago. I have not been able to even look at another woman— until the day you boarded the tour bus. Normally, I wouldn't even have taken such a tour. But I felt compelled to take it that day, to clear my head of some business concerns. I truly feel fate brought

us together, Samantha. And I intend to do everything in my power to make you see that also."

"But I'm not Anita—and I'm here with Jake."

"Be that as it may, I will never forgive myself if I don't do my best to win you."

Feroz's story melted Samantha. His loyalty was uncanny. She was quite flattered at being the recipient of such attention. But her heart was beating for Jake and yearning for his touch.

Samantha closed her eyes and drifted off again. As she surrendered to sleep, Feroz visited her in a dream.

The air in the room was thick with darkness, just like the place where she lay dreaming. Blood rushed through her veins as her heart pounded in response to the door creaking open. Moonlight scissored in, opening up the dark spaces. Shadows retreated. Feroz's hand reached out for hers. The mere brush of his skin excited her. Although she feared losing her mind to total surrender, she took his hand and followed him quietly. He walked her to the waters of the Ganges, with the moon smiling down at them. His passionate embrace was followed by a kiss that was both fierce and tender. Strong hands reached beneath her thin nightwear and caressed her body—grasping the fullness that responded. His eyes sought permission from hers. Her obvious longing made him undress her slowly, enjoying each stage of exposure. Having released her body from the captivity of garments, Feroz's voracious mouth began overwhelming her with bountiful pleasure. She moaned and whimpered, wanting him to anchor himself to her. Her hands guided him to luxuriate in her warm, inflamed womb. A surge of inseparable pleasure and pain overcame them and they became one in perfect bliss, uniting mind, body and soul.

But as she lay in Feroz's arms, inebriated from the forbidden pleasure, she experienced measureless guilt, knowing her heart belonged to Jake. Seagulls began circling above her, beating their wings and crying louder and louder with intense agitation. Waxing and waning waters soared to wash off her transgressions.

Samantha's penitence from the lifelike dream made her sinful body break out in a cold sweat. She sat up with a jolt in her bed—just like Jake had done many times before, desiring her.

CHAPTER ELEVEN

Morning broke. Pinkish rays forced their way through the barely open shutter slats in Samantha's room. A dark man sat at the foot of her bed. His facial features were barely identifiable, since the streak of dawn was behind him.

Samantha squinted her scarcely awake eyes to get a better look at him. His visage was still unclear, but his swarthy skin convinced her it was Feroz. She wondered if he had guarded her all night, contributing somehow to her wanton dream.

"Good morning, Sammy. It's really good to see you. I've missed you."

Surprised, Samantha inquired, "Jake? You look so dark that I almost mistook you for Feroz."

"That is what generally happens when the sun beats down at you for two days, frying your epidermis to a crisp."

"Two days? Has it been that long? I've been pretty much out of it. Tell me everything that happened."

"Having no leads, I took the two archaeology students Feroz made available to me and went on a camping trip—back to the stone figures. Conquering the monkeys was quite the task this time, since the team of lovers had been replaced by three men disturbing the amorous topography. But they seemed to give me the benefit of the doubt, once I bribed them with some bhang."

"Do go on, Jake."

"One by one, we checked beneath each of the lecherous males staring at the juvenile form, trying to discern her deserving counterpart. Knowing Norman, I should have guessed that he would have selected the most unlikely mate. But fool-

ishly, we wasted two days inspecting all others. The chosen male stood symbolically on the outside of the gathering, looking to where he had every right to be."

"What better way to say the deserving man will get the girl, despite being ostracized," added Samantha.

"Sam, you would have probably picked up on these subtleties the moment we got there, saving us loads of time and energy."

Samantha smiled at Jake's confidence in her. It was wonderful being around a man who wasn't shy to acknowledge her expertise over himself.

"So, what did you find?"

"The other half of the falcon, as we had expected, and a dusty old map."

"What is marked on the map, Jake?"

"That is what is so confusing about the whole damn thing. Absolutely *nothing* has been accented. I guess the falcon is supposed to guide us somehow."

"If we take our clues from superimposing one or both halves on the map, it might lead us somewhere."

"But how do we align them properly? The possibilities are endless, Sammy. We could spend a lifetime checking them out and still not find the right one."

"Jake, why is it that every time we uncover something, the end seems to slip farther and farther away from us?"

Jake took Sam into his arms, pulling her closer to his chest. There really wasn't much else he could do to reassure her. As he held her, he contemplated arranging a long overdue meeting with Princess Shanti, but thought better of telling Samantha, to avoid getting her hopes up.

Jake finally broke the unsettling silence. "I'm sorry, Sammy. I didn't mean to discourage you. It will all work out. It just has to. In the meantime, I say we enjoy our little adventure."

Having said that, Jake returned to his distracted state—his blank stare parted by a worried frown, while his eyebrows moved to the turning wheels in his mind.

"Penny for your thoughts, Jake."

"Nothing concrete yet. I would, however, like to excuse myself—to check on a couple of things."

Samantha started to get out of bed to ready herself for accompanying her partner in crime.

"Don't even think about it, Sammy. I'm not listening to you this time. You've barely recovered from your previous heroics. I refuse to let you toy with danger again. We're going to stick with Feroz's advice and give you a break."

"We've been in this together from the very beginning. You can't possibly start excluding me now, Jake."

"I wouldn't dream of it. But until you're feeling better, I'm going to insist that you let me do the legwork, while you try to make sense of the map situation."

"I suppose that sounds fair enough. But I'm warning you, Jake Alexander, you had better not be keeping anything from me. And that includes your whereabouts." Jake kissed Samantha on the forehead and darted out the door.

A clandestine meeting was arranged between Shanti and Jake at Mrs. Choudhry's office.

In speaking with the princess, Jake learned that Norman had kept her innocent as to the workings of his plans, for her security. But the little that Shanti knew, she unveiled—out of

steely determination to avenge the death of her one and only love.

Although Shanti felt her nugget of information was useless, it helped Jake ascertain that the trail to recovering the signet ring would have to begin at Kashmir. Proudly he raced to see Samantha, excited about sharing his newly discovered lead, like a child with a great report card after having feared the worst.

Jake jumped into the first available auto-rickshaw and announced the address of the Khan estate. The little cab made a few unusual turns into unfamiliar territory, and Jake realized something was wrong. By now, he knew enough of New Delhi to recognize that he was being taken to an alternative destination.

Frightfully, he yelled, "Stop right here! I've changed my mind! I want to be let out! I'll pay you full fare and then some, just stop immediately."

The driver gave Jake's pleas a deaf ear and continued on his mission. As the taxi dropped its speed to maneuver around a corner, Jake swiftly threw himself out of the doorless vehicle, landing headfirst on the filthy sidewalk, right next to the stagnant water in the drain beside it.

Jake's eyes opened to an ostentatiously done room, boasting typical Rajput-style decor. It looked like a room out of the Choudhry estate. A well-dressed man in his late fifties sat at the foot of his bed, glaring at him with concern and affection. As he moved closer, Jake noticed his strong Roman nose, silvery-gray hair, a matching mustache, and very fair skin.

"Where am I?" Jake inquired, looking around at his surroundings.

"Shhhh, my son. You must not waste your

energy talking. I assure you that you will be well taken care of."

"I guess so. But you still haven't told me where am I, or how I got here, for that matter."

"You are among family and friends. You were invited for a beautiful reunion, but you chose to fight. As a result, you had an accident and suffered a concussion."

"Unless I had a major memory loss—which I somehow doubt—I don't know what the hell you are talking about."

"Please don't be so hostile, my son. We—"

Rage tensed every single muscle on Jake's handsome face as his jugular pumped a hot pink flush into them.

"Stop calling me that!" he yelled.

The man patiently replied, "I don't blame you for being angry and hot-tempered. It's the Rajputana in you."

"I'm not a Rajput! I'm not even Indian! And until recently, I had never set foot on Indian soil."

"The man who bears the missing falcon has to be my son, whether he knows it or not."

As Jake looked up in shock, the silver-haired man continued. "I know that a grave injustice was done when your mother Kamani was kicked out by my wife, the Begum, after giving birth to you, my firstborn son. I would never have allowed such a deed, had I been around. But unfortunately, I was on a hunting trip that night. The *Begum* took full advantage of it, giving Kamani *manafsha*—a labor-inducing drink. It worked like a charm. You were born shortly after Kamani drank the potion. The *Begum* wanted the child to be born in my absence, right under my roof—to allow herself full control over 'handling' it. She felt it would be too risky to let Kamani give birth elsewhere. She could

have named me as the father on the records, bringing scandalous shame to the entire family. Immediately following the birth, both yourself and your mother were ousted, just as planned by the *Begum*. By the time I returned, it was too late. All that remained of the *Begum's* horrible plan was Kamani's body—claimed by suicide—and an unknown heir somewhere in an anonymous dwelling. I will never forgive the *Begum* for that—not for as long as I live."

The story came to an abrupt stop as the man wiped the tears rolling down his noble face. Undoubtedly, he was moved by what he was describing, and needed to steady his voice and reestablish his dignity before going any further. It was clear that he didn't want the facts to be fettered by his emotions.

Jake gathered that he was in the Rana palace, being mistaken for the long-lost Norman. But he pretended to know nothing of the tale he had just heard. After all, if he was working with the Choudhrys, they were adversaries.

Boldly, Jake spoke. "Look, mister, whoever you are, you're *not* my father—biologically or otherwise. I was born and raised in Queens, Canada. You can check my passport if you like. Now, if you'll just let me be on my way, you can search for your *real* son."

"Your fellow expeditionaries recognized the infamous falcon that Kamani had stolen for her illegitimate heir and informed me of your possession of it. That makes you my son."

"All that means is that I am an archaeologist who found a valuable masterpiece."

"But my sources also tell me that you have notes and diagrams pertaining to the omnipotent signet ring. The only way the two are related is through our family, *not* archaeology. And *that*, my boy, leads me to believe you have to be my son.

There is *no* other explanation."

Sarcastically, Jake replied, "Alas, the reason behind the sweet talk becomes clear. You think I have some powerful piece of jewelry that you need, and I will just hand it over to you, naturally, since all bonds have been reaffirmed."

"No, my son, that isn't it at all. But if that were the case, I do hope you would come through for your own flesh and blood."

Jake had to bite his tongue before he blurted out, "Like you came through for me," realizing he, too, had started thinking of himself as Norman.

Four days had passed since Jake's disappearance, leaving Samantha confused, frightened and distressed. She wondered if he had known about the valuable falcon all along and had accompanied her just to find it for selfish, materialistic reasons. It would certainly explain his departure, having located the treasure in its complete form. But her heart told her otherwise. And this time, despite Mrs. Fairchild's instructions, Samantha chose to listen to her heart.

The tragedy with Jake left Samantha alone, at Feroz's mercy. Despite his limited information, the man tried his best to help her. She could see that he weathered her anguish as if it were his own.

On the seventh day of futile searching, Samantha finally broke down and cried. She could no longer afford to keep Feroz in the dark, carrying the burden by herself. As she confessed every last detail of her plight, he cradled her head against his chest, soaking up her tears.

"I don't know what to do any more, Feroz. Only pure luck could help us now."

"Samantha, someone once said ninety-eight percent of good luck is hard work. Now that I know

your predicament, I'm going to see to it that I bring you that luck."

"Oh, Feroz, I wish that was all there was to it. I'm not even certain whether Jake is on my side and needs my help, or if I've been deliberately used and abandoned. It just sickens me to have such thoughts, but I have them nonetheless."

"I know in my heart that no man could know you and leave you. That leads me to believe that Jake is being held somewhere against his will, counting on us to free him. We simply can't afford to doubt him."

"I'm sure you're right, Feroz. I just hope something turns up soon."

CHAPTER TWELVE

"Keeping a secret in India is next to impossible. One can never do anything without everyone finding out about it. Servants love to gossip with other servants, who in turn enjoy divulging notable tales to their masters. Soon everybody finds out everything—and so will we. You just have to be patient, Samantha," said Feroz.

It wasn't long before the grapevine from the Ranas to the Khans brought news of the foreigner lodging there comfortably for the past eight days, enjoying overindulgent hospitality. Samantha was relieved that Jake was alive, but her stomach churned thinking about the possible implications of his pampered state. The actual probability of him being mistaken for Norman never once crossed her mind.

Feeling flustered, Samantha aired yet another series of doubts and reservations. Feroz cut in and convinced her that Jake was an innocent victim, being held for his valuable information. Samantha decided to accept that rationale, since it spoke to her head, not her heart.

Seeing her more settled, Feroz proceeded to philosophize.

"My dear Samantha. You must always remember—knowledge is easy, understanding difficult. With understanding comes absolute power, with misunderstanding powerful destruction. You alone can decide whether or not you want to admit the limitations of your understanding, and go on to help Jake and your ultimate goal. I do hope you choose based on what you can offer, not what is offered you."

Samantha began appreciating the wisdom that

Feroz was pouring out on her. She realized it wasn't really a choice that stood before her, since there was only one thing she could possibly do.

"Thank you, my wise friend. I'm ashamed that I consoled myself with self-pity, when I should have been thinking about helping Jake. Let's get started on planning his escape, without wasting any more time."

Since the critical news came forth from one of the Rana servants to a Khan domestic, Samantha and Feroz decided to enlist the help of the same duo in getting information back to Jake. A late-evening clandestine meeting was arranged.

Samantha and Feroz carefully outlined their strategy for getting Jake out the following night, right after dusk. According to the Rana servant, they couldn't have picked a better time. It coincided with a grand banquet. Hundreds of guests were expected, not to mention extra hired hands, from caterers to entertainers. Sneaking them into the confusion would be a cinch.

Money exchanged hands, and detailed plans for Jake were entrusted to the Rana steward. Samantha feared that the whole thing could blow up in their faces if he decided to change loyalties toward his employers. Feroz tried to reassure her otherwise. In either case, there was no backing out, since they lacked the luxury of alternatives.

Samantha tossed and turned all night long. Finding Jake was the only search that concerned her now; the falcon and the signet ring did not enter her mind.

The rosy glow of the rising sun was still below the horizon, birthing its way through the gray womb of darkness. Samantha sprang to her feet and started to get ready. The commotion in the bathroom woke Feroz, a little earlier than his usual time for morning prayers.

"Slow down, Samantha," was all he could say to keep her from bumping into him on her way back to the guest room.

"We have a very big day ahead of us. I can't afford to waste any time. You should get ready soon, too."

"I will, m'lady—all in good time. I don't want us to exhaust ourselves before we even make it to our mission. And trust me, it *will* happen, if you continue at this rate."

"I think I am too hyper to wind down *that* quickly."

"Why don't we start you off with a healthy breakfast, Samantha? I'm sure the good doctor has already told you what it can do for the rest of your day."

"Surely you jest, Feroz. I couldn't possibly stomach a thing."

"If I'm going to be taking care of you and helping you, I absolutely insist you take it a little easier."

"Okay, Feroz, but only if you will join me. We can certainly use a chance to go over our plans one more time."

"Now you're talking. Just give me a few minutes to wash up and finish with my prayers. We'll eat then."

Samantha felt it was time she herself got down on her hands and knees. Her shameful dream from the previous night tried to hinder her meditation, but she victoriously rose above it.

For the very first time since her ordeal started, Samantha was able to forgive Norman completely. Despite her worries, she experienced an unusual peace within herself. She didn't know if it was her spiritual state or her newfound friend's philosophies. In either case, the self-reflection did her good, shifting her focus to the larger picture.

As the evening drew near, Feroz presented Samantha with new native clothes and jewelry. He impressed upon her that if she was going to be a Rana guest, she had better dress the part.

"What happens if seating has been prearranged with place cards?"

"Have no such concerns. In India you just guesstimate your guest lists, because while some people may pull a no-show at the last minute, others will bring along friends and relatives to take their places. No one is ever turned away if they set foot in your house, wanting to break bread with you. No one. You don't even have to personally know your hosts."

"I guess I still have a lot to learn."

"I'd be more than happy to teach you all about our customs. But I must warn you, not all practices are as warm as the ones you might have been exposed to."

Samantha muttered to herself, "Don't I know it," reflecting on Norman's article, which had supposedly started it all.

Samantha and Feroz mingled beautifully into the crowds that packed the large cloistering tent beyond capacity. Round dining tables were covered with bright red tablecloths, matching the upholstery on the chairs. They contrasted with white cloth napkins, folded and starched to look like a flock of cockatoos, ready for a synchronized dance sequence. From the moment one stepped inside, all five senses were captivated with colorful sights, enchanting music, heady incense, and the general hustle and bustle of jostling crowds. But Samantha's mind had but one thought—Jake's escape. She was relieved when their nervous accomplice finally signaled them, and they headed out from the chaos, toward the mansion. As the threesome made their way to meet Jake at their pre-set destination, Samantha could have sworn she heard faint footsteps behind her. Fearfully, she turned her head to look over her shoulder. Four men in black-hooded cat suits—baring nothing but their eyes—lunged forward. Each grabbed one of her limbs while the accomplice restrained Feroz. Her bright-colored attire flapped like a butterfly as she put up an impressive struggle. Being no match for the professionals, her body eventually resigned. But her mind quickened, as questions raced through it. Who were these people? More importantly, who was behind them? Was it the Ranas, Jake, Feroz or someone else? What would anyone want from her anyway? Did they abduct Feroz as well—or worse, Feroz and Jake? Who could help her now? Could anyone be trusted?

Hearing the disturbance behind the rambling rose bushes, Jake leaped out from where he was hiding and started walking toward them. Tall trees formed a canopy that blocked the moon almost entirely. Jake could barely make out the figure of a curvaceous woman who stood with her back in his direction. Being certain that it was Samantha, Jake sneaked up behind her and proceeded to hug her excitedly. The woman turned around and laughed at him.

"Missed me *that* much?" she said, mockingly.

Jake was shocked that the woman was none other than Shanti Choudhry, with an angry glare flaming from her beautiful cat eyes.

"You're the last person I would have expected to see here. Aren't you supposed to stay away from the betrothed groom?"

"I could say the same for *your* presence, Jake Alexander—in a different context, of course. So, what exactly are you doing here? You couldn't possibly be thinking of double crossing us, could you?"

"Of course not. I'm a man of my word."

Jake nervously looked around for Samantha and Feroz.

"Afraid to be seen with me, Dr. Alexander?" Shanti said sarcastically.

"Don't be ridiculous. I'm just waiting for someone."

"And who might that be?"

"Not that it's any of *your* business, but I'm waiting for Samantha and a good friend. They are supposed to help me get out of here."

Shanti clapped her hands three times. "Bravo! You're very clever—leading me to believe that you're being held against your wishes by the people you marched to, straight from our little meeting."

"I was abducted."

"Likely story. But I'm neither a fool nor one to take any chances. So I'm going to see to it that you leave with me right now, to fulfill your promise to my people."

"And what makes you think that I'll just walk away, leaving Samantha waiting in a potentially dangerous situation, worrying about me?"

"I wouldn't be too concerned about that, if I were you. She won't be coming. I've been told that she is indisposed."

"What are you talking about, Shanti?"

"You heard me. Being a smart man, you figure it out."

With horror in his eyes, Jake gasped, "Oh my gosh! Finding me here, you must have thought I was working with the Ranas! You've shanghaied Samantha as a way of ensuring that I keep my end of our bargain. But I swear to you, I did *no* such thing. You must believe me! I was truly abducted. I hadn't even met the Ranas up until then." Folding his hands in a prayer-like fashion, Jake went on to plead, "Please. Release Samantha."

"I never said she was with us. And even if she was, what makes you think I would just let her walk away, with you being mysteriously cozied away at the Ranas?"

"If I was voluntarily 'cozied away at the Ranas'— as you put it—would I need to sneak around like this to escape?"

"Look, Jake, I don't know what games you're playing, or on which teams for that matter, but I'm going to make sure I protect my family's interests."

"I'm *not* playing any games! As for which 'team' I intend to help, it's you, as soon as I can get out of here—which incidentally may not take place if you waste any more of my time. Now, I insist you let me leave, *immediately!*"

Jake and Shanti's argument grew louder, attracting the night watchmen—*chauki-daar.* The quarrelsome duo hurriedly jumped the wall that fenced the property and landed in a throng of prickly *Keekar* shrubs. Sharp thorns tore skin and clothes alike, making the two bodies appear as if they had just survived a wrestling match with a wild beast. For Shanti, the insinuations appeared to be even worse—with a half-stripped body.

Jake began removing the thorns from Shanti's tender skin—all the while wondering how it was possible for her to be so shrewd with him, when she was nothing more than a terrified trembling mess in her mother's presence. It attested to his knowledge of Indian parents being able to control their children, demanding family loyalty over personal goals.

Having removed the last of the thorns, Jake wiped the scratches on Shanti's face with his shirt. The look in the cat eyes softened toward him, as did the tone in the previously harsh voice. Jake hoped that she might release some information on Samantha, after all. But that was an entirely different story. All that Jake knew was that he had been cautioned. His only consolation was that the doting Mr. Khan was with Samantha—or at least knew something about her disappearance.

CHAPTER THIRTEEN

Feroz lay motionless on the unlit forest floor. Despite its dense ceiling, the jungle left its doors wide open to mosquitoes and other parasites. Finding Feroz defenseless, the insects ravaged his body. He could feel their stings when he woke from his temporary stupor. But it paled in comparison to the sharp, raw pain that sliced through the right side of his forehead. Feroz realized that he had sustained a cranial injury, one serious enough to claim his consciousness. Feeling disoriented, he tried to lift himself off the lumpy ground.

As he steadied himself on his feet, Feroz looked at the city in the distance. He could see that its twinkling Christmastree-like form had changed to the last few cinders of a dying fireplace. Feroz gathered it was the middle of the night. Although the quiet all around gave the illusion of calm, terror savagely gouged away at his valor. His body felt cold, his bowels soft, as he tried to recollect the events that led up to his current state. But his recent memory failed him miserably.

Feroz chose to ignore the blackness that swallowed everything, dead or alive, and started to make his way out of the wooded tunnel, focusing only on the dim lights at its very end. As he dragged himself out of the grove, the moon struggled out from behind heavy clouds and beamed down an approving smile—signaling its vow to guide him to the safety of the walled city. Feroz felt the world about him spin crazily as his strength ebbed away, but he sauntered down the silvery slope nonetheless.

After an endless walk, Feroz finally made it back to civilization. His crown throbbed, while all uncovered areas of his skin itched and burned.

Exposed nerves screamed from pain as blood oozed out to smother them.

Feroz caught his reflection in a mirrored store window. The man that looked back no longer wore a light suit or a handsome face. A sizable laceration above his right brow swelled his visage—converting it to a purple, unrecognizable mass—while his garments turned crimson from soaking in blood. Feroz realized that he needed immediate professional help. There was no telling what kind of infections he may have already been exposed to.

Finding a cab at that time of the night was challenging, but not impossible—unless, of course, the passenger was a ghost-like figure, drenched in blood, looking more frightening than the nocturnal creatures which haunt the streets at that hour.

Feroz staggered and reeled aimlessly, until his weak body gave in to the demands of his injury, and he fell limp to the ground.

A loud startling bang clamored through Feroz's head as the hospital doors were pushed open by the front end of his stretcher. He opened his swollen eyes to a brilliant glare, beaming down from the fluorescent ceiling.

A series of tests, X-rays, examinations and injections followed, once the delicate handiwork of sewing up the facial wound was complete. As uncomfortable as Feroz was, the optimist in him focused only on his good fortune—another half an inch lower and he would have lost sight in his right eye.

The hospital staff wanted to keep Feroz for observation, since he had no idea how long he had been unconscious, either of the two times. But he refused and made his way out, crying, "Anita needs me."

Having said that, he frightened himself, knowing that he had not seen Anita for two decades. He wondered if he had lost his mind, or the last twenty years of his life—having no memory of them. Realizing that his time frame remained intact, Feroz decided it couldn't be the latter.

Feroz's questions were answered sooner than he thought possible. Upon his return home, he was greeted by a team of worried family members and Jake. Seeing Jake and sharing in a brief conversation with him jogged his memory. He realized that it was Anita's look-alike, Samantha—not Anita herself—who needed his help. Instantly, he promised his assistance to Jake.

Mrs. Khan, his elderly mother, looked on very unhappily. She swept the room with her chilled gaze. Feroz knew that as upset as she was at his condition, and recognized it could get worse before getting better, she would keep her mouth shut—knowing how he had blamed her for losing the love of his life. Not wishing to squander time, the two men sat down together and began comparing notes. Jake became enraged when he heard about Samantha's complete disclosure to Feroz. But as Feroz described how tormented she had been during his absence, and offered a few helpful ideas of his own, Jake expressed relief at having him share the burden.

Feroz asked his sisters to do a complete makeover on his friend. A white lurban, native cotton garb and a fake mustache were used to transform Jake's exterior.

Having completed the metamorphosis, Jake gave himself a once-over in the mirror and smiled. "That ought to blend me into the crowds inconspicuously."

"For now, anyway. But you must never drop your guard, my friend. The stakes are too high.

They *will* find you, sooner than you think."

Feroz noticed an apprehensive expression on Jake's face. It seemed to go beyond worrying about the Ranas.

"Are you going to stand there and daydream all day long? Or are you going to join me in our rescue mission for Samantha?"

As one might have expected, the two men headed straight for the Choudhrys. This time, the gatekeepers let them in without hesitation. Mrs. Choudhry greeted them at the door. "We've been expecting you, Dr. Alexander. Please, *do* come in."

Having seated them, she busied herself with summoning the servants to prepare a high tea for her guests.

"This is *not* a social visit. Let's just get on with it," Jake said, irritated.

"One must never forget to show hospitality. It's bad luck."

Jake let out a sarcastic laugh. "You amuse me, Mrs. Choudhry. You don't honestly believe that a tea will change your luck after having kidnapped an innocent victim and hurting my friend Feroz the way you have—do you?"

"I claim no such responsibility."

"Then why were you expecting us?" inquired Jake.

"Shanti told me about your accusations last night."

"Did Shanti also happen to mention that *she* is the one who informed me of Samantha being indisposed in the first place?"

"I guess I do owe you an explanation for that one. You see, Dr. Alexander, a lot of people would like to rectify the mess that Norman Fairchild created. It has grave implications for all involved. We can't afford any slip-ups—like one side or the other

inheriting the powerful ring, subsequently default-
ing on the agreement. A third party, outside the
two dynasties, decided to intervene in good faith—
being a friend to both sides. *They,* my friends, are
responsible for Samantha's disappearance. Their
goal is to right a wrong by restoring the Rajputana
royalty, and accumulating good karma for themselves in the process. So, you see, you needn't fear
any harm to Samantha. They only have good in-
tentions at heart."

Jake muttered to Feroz, "Just like they didn't
hurt you."

Following a brief pause, Jake composed himself and continued, with cold menace still in his
voice, "I refuse to start my mission without
Samantha. Send your goons with us if you like—
you know, to promote 'trust.' But I don't intend to
leave without her."

Having said that, Jake put up his feet on the
divan and made himself comfortable. Feroz gathered it was to emphasize that he meant every word.

Reluctantly, Mrs. Choudhry got on the phone
and relayed the situation to her alleged 'third
party'—but without a twinge of compassion.

Two cups of tea later, Samantha stood, unharmed, in the doorway. Feroz and Jake jumped
to their feet, tears blurring their vision. One by
one, she hugged them—squeezing hard with intense emotion. Feroz noticed Jake's nostrils flare
as he took a deep breath to disguise the jealousy
flitting across his eyes. It was a look all too familiar to him, from all the times he himself had
yearned to be in Jake's shoes, with Samantha's
excited body plastered against his. Feroz stepped
back and began talking about the intense fear her
truancy had incited.

The threesome was lead out of the estate as a

foursome—with an armed guard tagging along. Jake made it very clear from the outset that their escort was only allowed to follow at a safe distance, without *ever* becoming party to any activity or conversation. "Speak only when you are spoken to," was the rule of thumb.

Feroz encouraged Jake to settle his bill at the Oberoi and move himself and Samantha into the Khan estate—for safety and economics, among other reasons. There was certainly room enough, considering only four people inhabited the eight-bedroom estate built around the memorable courtyard Samantha and Jake had already had the pleasure of enjoying. Feroz made the offer even more tempting by pointing out the comfort of sumptuous home-cooked meals and attentive servants.

Having their acceptance to his invitation, Feroz instructed his servants to freshen up and ready their rooms for an indefinite stay. As they drove from the hotel to the Khans', Jake informed them that the next clue was to be found in Kashmir—the lovers' capital.

Feroz smiled and said, "I have to hand it to Norman—the man really had a flair for picking his sites. I can certainly think of worse places to be stuck in than a paradise that has held the fascination of millions—Bernier in the sixteen hundreds, to name one."

Samantha added, "A land so extraordinaire that its bracing beauty and legends capture the very soul of romance."

The trip to Srinagar, the capital of Kashmir, was planned for early morning the following day.

Feroz showed Jake and Sam to separate guest rooms at opposite ends of the hall and said, "We must turn in early in preparation for tomorrow's journey. I will wake you up at the crack of dawn."

Having taken turns disappearing, Sam became convinced of her love and desire for Jake. Sensing similar emotions from him, she had hoped for a touching and passionate reunion, but was denied, as it was against traditional rules.

Somewhere between the goodnights and the clock's twelve chimes, Samantha decided to end her restless tossing and turning and started to make her way to Jake's room. She would have virtually bumped into him—with him heading her way—if it weren't for the moonlight streaming in, bathing the balcony hallway with its milky white beam.

Samantha grabbed Jake's hand and sneaked him into her room and under her sheets. They felt as mischievous as adolescents enjoying abandon in the absence of supervision.

As Jake started to kiss and touch her expertly, Samantha closed her eyes to the world and focused solely on their pleasurable union. An excited commotion shook her imagination, without words once taking part. She felt like they were touching for the very first time.

Samantha let out a big moan in response to the sex that tormented her mind and body. Hearing her pain, Feroz woke up and ran to her deliverance, only to find her in the arms of another man. A deep emotional pang radiated from his heart to the rest of his body, like a darting tongue of lightning. Not being able to endure it, he wanted to leave. But his feet froze, being struck by the sensuality of the unplanned voyeurism. As the images branded themselves into his memory, he could feel the burning pain of each impression. But despite his distress, his gaze could not escape her. A cacophony of groans, screams and shrieks caused the blood in his veins to rush—spinning his head with delight, but whipping the stiffness in his pants with torturous pain. Jealousy awakened in him, bringing with it intolerable doubts about his future self-restraint. He knew if he didn't depart right then and there, envy at not being the one plunging into her would totally consume him. But then she climaxed and glanced flirtatiously at him—exuding desire and fascination.

CHAPTER FOURTEEN

The picturesque bus ride into Srinagar unfolded a panoramic view of the most beautiful topography imaginable. Samantha stared at the breathtaking scenery whizzing by like a perfectly shot documentary. The only way she could be certain that it was real was through the garden-fresh scent being transported by the breeze. The fragrance reached a peak beyond compare when the bus passed by the enchanting saffron fields—unduplicated anywhere else in the world, despite endless attempts. Samantha couldn't help but poke her head out the window to inhale their intoxicating smell.

She continued to be amazed as her eyes followed vistas of snow-clad mountain tops leading down into meadows carpeted with flowers. Rock formations sculpted by mother nature and highlighted by tumbling waterfalls and streams punctuated the never-ending span of earthly delights.

Knowing that Feroz was a learned man, Samantha urged him to share the history and legends of the simple but spellbinding land.

Proudly, Feroz reported, "I must warn you both that Kashmir is the ultimate region for love and romance. Honeymooning couples the world over have testified to its inescapable supernatural charms."

Samantha smiled and said, "Must be the magic of the world-famous gardens."

"They were laid out in the early sixteen hundreds by Emperor Jehangir for his wife Nur Jahan, to celebrate his love for her beauty," added Feroz.

As the bus drove into town, Samantha was completely taken by the colorful markets that adorned both sides of the road. Vendors shouting their wares, and customers haggling, drew her just as much as the goods at the center of the commotion. She wanted to get out of the bus, mingle and buy it all—exotic fruits, vegetables, hand-embroidered fabrics and papier-mache crafts.

Feroz laughed and said, "Slow down, Samantha. You haven't seen anything yet. Delayed gratification might just work to your advantage this time."

As the threesome made their way out of the colorful bus, they noticed their sentry wasn't too far behind.

Looking at him, Jake said, "This is truly nauseating. Let's check into a hotel he can't afford—to put a comfortable distance between us."

Feroz raised his eyebrows and said, "Hotel? No, no, my friend. One can not experience Kashmir unless one lives aboard a houseboat. They were started when the maharajahs forbade foreigners to own land in their beautiful empire. According to the Europeans, living aboard them is the consummate way to vacation—with an enchantment that Venice can barely approximate. You're constantly surrounded by a dazzling display of lotuses, spangled in the waters. Their bracing beauty is perhaps the most striking in all of the wilderness."

Enthusiastically, Samantha said, "Sounds heavenly."

"You have my vote also, since it's bound to shake off our unwelcome guard," added Jake.

"Very well, then. You both wait here while I make all the arrangements. Seeing foreigners has a way of inflating prices," smiled Feroz.

The leisurely pace in Kashmir slowed down Samantha and Jake right at the outset. They decided to start their mission the following morning, devoting the remainder of the day to laid-back planning.

Feroz returned with papers confirming the rental of the most beautiful three-bedroom house-

boat he could find. It came complete with a servant who minded the boat, cooked, cleaned, tended
bar and helped bargain with merchants in
shikaras—small boats selling everything from food
and postage to skillful handicrafts.

As the rooster crowed its morning cock-a-doo-
dle-doo, Samantha woke up, feeling unrested. She
remarked that the night dwindled far too quickly—
plunging them headfirst into confronting the real
reason for their voyage. Breakfast awaited, as did
the tattered map—with half a falcon aligned on it.

Jake said, "Shanti informed me that Norman
always spoke of Kashmir as a falcon's eye, and
the various rivers and streams that flow from it as
the lines in its wings. Now, the million dollar question is—if Kashmir is the bull's eye for our next
clue, where exactly is it hidden?"

What followed was a couple of hours of intelligent and not-so-intelligent deliberations and
guessing—without any results. The mysterious eye
continued to be mysterious, while the map barely
escaped being torn apart by Jake's hands.

Samantha finally suggested, "Let's turn to a local guru and seek advice on the most romantic and
passionate site—in keeping with Norman's style."

"In a place like Kashmir? It would be easier
to find a needle in a haystack," added Jake sarcastically.

Feroz jumped to Samantha's rescue. "You'd be
surprised at what the wise men can tell us. Their
ways are pure and unclouded."

"Sounds quite the opposite to what might have
appealed to dear Norman... In either case, I guess
it's worth a try," grunted Jake.

Feroz went to the front of the boat, where the
servant was diligently guiding the sizable craft

through lily pads and early morning retailers. Samantha observed an extensive conversation— mumbled in their native language. It was concluded by the turning of the large vessel onto a new course.

Following a fair journey, the houseboat docked in a beautiful, out-of-the-way lagoon. Feroz helped Samantha and Jake ashore.

As the little team walked up winding dirt roads, strewn with colorful rocks and pebbles, the Choudhry escort tagged along. His bulging eyes and knees kept pace with them, although his cut and callused heels begged to slow down.

The hour-and-a-half-long uphill hike ended at a small humble hut, belonging to a holy man. The door was left ajar, seemingly to welcome people into his presence. Jake's hand moved up reflexively to knock on the portal, but Feroz pulled it back.

"We mustn't disturb him. We'll just take a seat inside and wait for him to address us when he is ready."

Samantha looked around at the stark, claustrophobic shack. A floor mat, an earthenware pitcher with water, a couple of handmade, rough wooden chairs and a holy book were all that it contained. Its simplicity matched its feeble inhabitant's minimal attire—a *dhoti* and a Lucknow cap, to cover his loins and head respectively.

Following a few moments of prayerful pacing, the guru invited them to speak. All secrets were disclosed to him, so they could benefit fully from his wisdom.

The pious creature sat down on the floor mat, with arms and legs crossed and eyes shut. His mouth began to chant as he entered into meditation, before giving his advice.

Feroz whispered, "This particular creed of people are chaste and unpretentious, with dishonesty never touching their lives. They have their own laws and refrain from the use of currency. Money is seen as evil, since it puts a price on things God gave to us to enjoy. Barter is the prevalent form of acquiring goods. All necessities are seen as having equal value."

"Then how will we repay him for his services?" asked Jake.

"Wisdom is an unmatched entity. It's only given to those who will put the knowledge to good use," replied Feroz.

By now, the learned being had completed his contemplation, and invited the whispering group to sit down on the floor mat with him. He began his speech by saying, "The falcon generally symbolizes a bird of prey, known for hunting and killing. But the falcon that your friend had represented immortality. It would appear that he chose it deliberately to make his name and creed immutable. The only place that could guard his name in the face of outstanding annihilators would be Kashmir's largest mosque—the Jama Masjid. Raised by a sultan in the thirteen hundreds, it has managed to survive three ravaging fires—despite its roof being solely supported by a wooden framework of three hundred cedar trunks. Go to it, and look for his name in the ancient timber."

Feroz half-bowed before the holy man and said, "How do we ever pay you back for your insight?"

"If you protect the honor you have set out to preserve, doing the best you can, your deeds will be a great reward. Go to your task now, with strength and courage—fighting all distractions, temptations and fears. Give yourselves only to love, and to your cause."

Feroz, Samantha and Jake folded their hands together, bade farewell, and started their trek back. Going down the slopes took only half the time, since hope, gravity and cooler temperature worked in their favor.

"It's starting to look better, Sammy."

"If I were you, I wouldn't get too hopeful, Jake. Norman appears to have made the search progressively harder—the more we learn, the lesser we seem to know."

Feroz cut in. "Stop, you two. The scholar told us not to lose courage. We must press on, without wasting our energy on useless bickering."

"You're right," the couple recited simultaneously.

The team boarded the houseboat, which then turned around gracefully and swam like a swan back to its nighttime resting place in Dal Lake.

The hustle and bustle at the banks at nightfall sharply contrasted with the peaceful seclusion of the daytime adventure. But it held its own allure, nonetheless, with crowded restaurants bordering the boulevard near the boat sanctuary. Feroz indicated that any one of them would do, since each was known for its variety of sumptuous Kashmiri foods, romantic atmosphere and pampering service.

As this was their first official conquest together, Feroz planned a celebration, accentuating the Kashmiri enchantment through a memorable evening. An exquisite outdoor dinner under the stars and antique cafe lamps was followed by a promenade into town. A colorful *tonga—caleche—* took them for a ride through the hamlet, highlighting local arts and entertainment.

Samantha noticed a regional embroidered

outfit with a matching veil, bejeweled with coin-like charms, displayed in a storefront window. Immediately, her mind wandered to how it might look on her, helping her create a one-woman harem for Jake. She decided to purchase it first thing the following morning. Little did she know the outfit was already spoken for—same model, different buyer.

The houseboat awaited its guests with a beautifully decorated deck. Lit lanterns adorned its railings. The movement of the waves swayed them from side to side. Samantha walked up to one of them and began admiring the intricate detail on its frame. Jake sneaked up behind her and wrapped his arms around her shoulders, pulling her closer to himself. A gentle breeze started to breathe invigorating, exhilarating freshness onto their faces. Its life-giving caress blew a curl into one of Samantha's eyes. Jake tenderly brushed it back with his long, tapered fingers, and secured it in place with a little kiss.

Samantha melted into Jake's arms, her skin dissolving into his. Her movements were provocative and suggestive. Feroz noticed the exchange of sensual warmth that took place between them. It enflamed his desire to the point of covetous madness. His ever-present imagination returned—to punish her this time—thrusting hard into her, putting an end to her 'teasing.' He had to have her, if only once. He believed its memory could suffice for a lifetime. He could never again experience tranquillity otherwise. No one else could take her place—perhaps because she herself was filling in for someone else.

Feroz noticed Jake looking at him with an insurmountable uneasiness—man to man, predator to predator.

"I think we should call it a night," Jake suggested hurriedly.

The threesome concluded an unspoken conversation, with glances and body language directing them to their respective rooms.

CHAPTER FIFTEEN

Three hundred pillars, aged more than six centuries each, representing a total accumulation of one hundred and eighty millennia—awaited to be scrupulously examined by three lost souls. The magnificent overbearing structure that they upheld gave a secure feeling of what lay within, but the skepticism of the little squad made them insecure nonetheless.

As the threesome arrived at the main gate and took off their shoes out of respect, Jake instructed, "Since there really doesn't appear to be any method to Norman's madness, why don't we divide up the colonnades into three sections—making each of us responsible for a hundred."

"I agree," added Samantha. "There is no other conceivable way of getting through such an enormous task."

"Seeing that it may take us all day, why don't we agree to meet back here at one, for lunch," Feroz suggested.

In agreement, the three comrades went their separate ways.

Despite the shade of the formation, the heatwave made the place almost unbearable. But the persistent crew pressed on. Samantha was especially engrossed in reading every crack and line—so much so that she dismissed the shadow lurking behind the grand columns in her vicinity as nothing more than a heat and fatigue related hallucination.

Two hours into her inspection, Samantha started to feel faint from dehydration. Her delicate, sensitive form was never one to stand heat very well—not being acclimatized to significantly higher temperatures especially made it worse. Feeling the onset of dizziness, followed by inevitable darkness, Samantha stopped dead in her tracks and took support from the post she was examining.

A well-dressed man in his late forties popped out of nowhere and offered Samantha his assistance. She was relieved, being noticed by someone in her desolate corner.

"Allow me to assist you, madam," from the stranger, and "Thank God you're here," from herself, were the last things Samantha remembered hearing before the tornado of unconsciousness sucked her in.

Samantha's eyes finally opened onto a group of unfamiliar female faces, staring inquisitively from beneath unwimpled *burkas*—black headcovers with veils. Samantha gave a gracious smile and thanked them for the rescue.

Realizing it was three o'clock already, Samantha got up briskly from the futon that had been used to make her comfortable. She wanted to rush to Jake and Feroz before they became insane with worry. But the oldest of the ladies forced her back down onto the futon, while the other ladies started to clap and hum in a ritualistic manner.

Samantha tried to resist her overly accommodating hosts, but her efforts were futile. She was clearly outnumbered.

Confused by the situation, she finally inquired, "Would someone mind explaining to me what is going on? I feel fine now, and would really like to leave. There are people who must be worried sick about me."

The ladies cackled and began undressing her, without responding to her question. Samantha furiously tried to clutch her clothes, holding them forcefully onto her body.

"What the hell do you think you are doing? I'm a Canadian citizen! You can't treat me like this!"

An elderly patrician, whose face announced her life experiences by the hundreds of folds etched into it, finally started conversing with Samantha.

"My dear lady, your laws are no good here. The sultan has honored you by choosing you as his next bride. His word is the law. Consider yourself fortunate, and prepare to make sure you awaken his desire. Do not disappoint him."

"You can't just kidnap me, assuming that I'm single and want to be married."

"The sultan did not kidnap you—he merely delivered you from loneliness and hard work, since you found favor in his eyes."

"But I'm already with someone, and you've dragged me here against my wishes."

All the ladies in the room giggled—as if they had never heard such an absurdity.

The elderly woman continued, "If you truly belonged to someone, he would not have left you alone like that. He would have made sure you were accompanied, if he himself was unable to do it. You could have died out there if it wasn't for the sultan."

"You misunderstand. I am on a job. My teammates were with me in the mosque, working in different areas."

"That is the second thing you were fortunate enough to be liberated from—labor. The sultan felt a beautiful creature like you should never again have to soil her hands or tire her body with hard work. From now on, you will be constantly pampered. Your only concern will be to look disarming."

"How can you live powerlessly like this—belonging to someone else?"

The elderly lady laughed amusedly at

Samantha's philosophy of life and said, "Don't you know that the very power a man struggles all his life to obtain can be snatched from him in a moment by a beautiful woman—to use and direct as she pleases? Her loveliness can enslave him to carry out her wishes and commands. A bright woman would never take such an opportunity lightly."

"I would like to be responsible for my own power! I do not wish to become a femme fatale at someone else's expense. Now, if you'll just let me go, we'll call this kidnapping nothing more than a big misunderstanding—no hard feelings."

The maiden-in-charge became indignant and shouted, "That is not for you to decide!" and signaled a crew of ladies by snapping her fingers.

Samantha's sundress was removed from her body. She quivered shamefully in her knickers as a harem of twenty or so women watched her naked, porcelain skin get rubbed down with perfumed lotions and potions.

Next, Samantha's scented frame was lowered into a steaming concrete tub—much like a Turkish bath. Thirty-foot-high arched pillars surrounded it—each bejeweled with magnificent patterns made out of colorful miniature tiles, rocks, beads and mirrors. Watching Samantha's apprehension, a few of the harem girls joined her in the relaxing bath—supposedly to make her feel comfortable with the sisterhood. Still others welcomed her with smiles and ceremonial songs.

Having been kidnapped recently as a bargaining chip was bad enough, but at least the right tradeoff promised a way out of it. Being seized as a personal possession promised no such hope.

Samantha felt truly despondent, but she was too numb and terrified to do anything about it. She decided to turn her mind off the experience and go along with the game—at least until she could come up with an alternative plan. One thing was for certain—she knew she was in it alone. Her fellow harem girls would have no sympathy for her. To them, she was being "honored" by the marriage. After all, the sultan could have chosen to just take her by force, enslaving her as a concubine, without being concerned about her integrity—something they were convinced girls from the West lacked anyway, since they didn't appear to view their chastity as a precious commodity.

Although Samantha had read about the different ideology, ad nauseam, being exposed to them firsthand stunned her. But she was in no position to pass judgment or turn the females against what they considered acceptable and desirable.

Samantha's retreat into her psyche was abruptly ended when she was pulled out of the bath. Her body was dried in a luxuriously plush towel, soft, to protect her flesh. Next, an inner core of ladies removed her knickers and shaved her pubic hair, to furnish her for Muslim consumption.

Natural dyes in various colors were brought in to "prepare" her. The painting ceremony began, with intricate patterns being drawn in henna on her palms, soles and nipples. Once washed—after the proper drying process—they were to leave beautiful burnt-orange artistry on her skin. Following the henna craftsmanship, pure kohl was used to highlight her eyes, while rose blush and scarlet lipstick were employed to accentuate her cheeks and mouth.

Her body was then covered in the exquisite attire she had noticed in the window the night before. Once her veil was lowered—as a final touch—she was completely covered from head to toe, baring only her eyes.

Two obese eunuchs approached to escort her to her groom. Samantha sobbed profusely, hoping that they would notice her reluctance and somehow save her from having to participate in the planned ordeal.

Being a disinterested bride for a second time in her life appalled Samantha—even more so this time, since consummation seemed inevitable.

Samantha stood, trembling, in a large room that epitomized the brink of decadence. Her eyes followed the intricacies, from rare Persian rugs on the floor and erotic tapestries on the walls, right up to the gilded vaulted ceilings—all combining arresting colors and textures. But their beauty paled in comparison to the adjoining garden that drew Samantha to itself, via its inviting crushed sandstone walkway. It was alive with a fresh scent of jasmine and the distinctive sounds of haunting sitar music. The flower beds boasted rare breeds, with effervescent fountains at their nuclei. Their sprays snaked like meandering ribbons. Colorful lights danced within them, making each sparkling drop appear like a precious gem.

While Samantha looked around in amazement, she caught someone appraising her like a slave at an auction. Despite his drastic change of attire, she recognized the brawny, handsome figure as he came forward and stood before her. Purple silk *shalwar kameez*, golden brocade robe and magenta turban replaced the formal suit from earlier on in the day.

Without a word, he stared into her eyes for the longest time. Then he said, "I like what I see."

With trembling lips, Samantha mouthed, "How can you say that? You don't even know me! And all you can see of me are my eyes!"

"They are all I need to see, since they are windows into the soul. They can conquer, defeat, control—but never lie. Looking into them, without any distractions from the rest of the woman's beautiful form, is the only way to wisely select a mate. Your eyes tell me that I've chosen judiciously. Yes, indeed."

"Does it not matter to you that the choice is not mutual?"

Shock flooded the sultan's face. With eyes gaping almost as extensively as his wide-open mouth, he replied, "No one has *ever* disagreed with the sultan's choice before! But if you are bold enough to tell me otherwise, I shall simply have to defer the obvious until you choose me of your own free will. And you *will* choose me—I'm convinced of it. I wouldn't want you any other way. I need to be certain that you are delighted with the honor bestowed upon you—just like any other woman in your place would be. But the time I offer you must remain our secret. My people will mock me and not respect me if they find out that, despite my power, I let you have your way."

Samantha was beginning to understand what the wise woman had told her about overpowering the most omnipotent of creatures with female wiles. The sultan threw back his beefy shoulders, grabbed his strong chin, and continued, "We will go through with the wedding as planned, but you will stay in your own quarters—adjacent to mine—mingling with me in my private courtyard and during mutually agreed upon jaunts. The conjugal consummation will only take place when you're ready for the honor, and look forward to giving yourself to me."

Grateful for the privilege extended her, Samantha played along. She bowed before the sultan, kissed the hem of his robe, and offered her gratitude, "Thank you, my lord. You are very kind."

The revelry lasted two additional days, with celebrations involving a throng of women, children and eunuchs—ranging from the sovereign *begum*, wives, relatives, concubines and ladies-in-waiting, all the way to guards and slaves. What followed was the commemoration of a divine courtship—full of masterful charm and affection.

Samantha's private boudoir was a treat in itself. The floor was completely covered with fine Persian carpets, matching the sultan's. Their craftsmanship competed with the Kashmiri tapestries that cloaked every last inch of the towering walls. The look was completed with a domed ceiling, blanketed with intricate, hand-painted patterns. Samantha was hard-pressed to close her eyes to such a gallery of talent.

Each day began with the sultan's handmaiden bringing in a basket of royal treats for the new bride—fresh fruits, flowers, scented bath oils, exquisite clothes, and a handwritten invitation by the sultan, requesting her company in exotic plans. The presentation was followed by a morning bath and step-by-step assistance in making Samantha feel pampered and beautiful—as much as she loathed the useless ritual. She ranked it with all the other activities used to sugarcoat the glorified prison that robbed freedom, and confined its inhabitants by the use of purdah.

Excursions ranged from picnics accompanied by intoxicating sarod music to hunting expeditions through sublime jungles.

Transportation was limited to leisurely rides aboard decorated elephants with umbrella canopies. The gray beasts never failed to fascinate Samantha, with their curling and uncurling trunks, long ivory tusks, fanning ears, and heavy feet—shaking the earth beneath with a laboring force that caused them to pant, huff and puff incessantly.

The adventure and excitement of each trip was further spiced by the sizzle of flattering comments, sensual admiration and romantic poetry, created for the bride by the groom.

Physical contact was limited to the sultan kissing Samantha's hand each time he assisted her on or off the elephant saddle.

At nightfall, dinner and entertainment in the sultan's personal courtyard were invariably concluded by the presentation of a precious gift to Samantha, hand-picked by the sultan himself.

CHAPTER SIXTEEN

The new moon grew from blackness to full radiance, completing an entire cycle. Calendars progressed. The sultan persisted in squandering his affection on Samantha.

But Samantha dared not budge from her position and go to the great man out of her own choice—not that she hadn't been tempted on several occasions. His power was intoxicating, his love mesmerizing, his refuge seductive. Guilt dominated her—for desiring as well as holding back. Part of her wished he would negate their arrangement, absolving her of the responsibility. But her heart wouldn't allow her to suggest it—even subliminally—for it remained loyal to Jake. Furthermore, she couldn't just forget the two tormented loves who must still be continuing their thwarted search for her—their ultimate treasure—and the signet ring.

The fair maiden and her handsome escort went on their usual pre-sunset horseback ride. Only this time they rode until their shadows went from growing longer and longer to being completely engulfed by the luminous full moon. The atmosphere about them sang an omen to the unusual night that was sure to follow. The sultan ended his sumptuous dinner by imbibing a feast of fine wines, despite Islamic abstinence. His eyes grew heavier with inebriation, and his inhibitions broke down one by one—until finally one last quaff pushed him across the line between being a man of his word to a man ruled by love.

Throwing back his head to sip the last drop from his silver goblet, the sultan began speaking without restraint.

"The time has come that you learn a few things,

Samantha. From the moment I laid eyes on you, I fell in love with you. Initially, it was physical, but through our courtship, it has grown in many ways. Each day I spend with you, I'm charmed by learning that your values are different from all others with, who hunger only for what I represent. They waste their time in idle pleasures, preening themselves, all in the hopes of being called unto me. Once summoned, they come due to rank, as pawns with artifices—all with a price—making me impotent. You, however, have reawakened my desires and brought radiance to my soul—thereby becoming a challenge. You constantly fill my thoughts—making me desire you more and more desperately each day. So much so, that I'm afraid if you make me wait any longer, I might not be able to keep myself from you."

Samantha knew that the man spoke fairly. She also wanted the situation resolved, one way or another. She had come away empty each time she tried to devise a solution for her escape—from the onerous guard and the emotional turmoil.

Samantha concluded her contemplations by seductively suggesting, "If it pleases the sultan, I say we play a game or a bet. If you win, I shall proudly reward you with my womanhood, by becoming your wife in *every* way. But if *I* win, you must release me—immediately—to continue on with my life."

"Very well. Tomorrow at dawn you will go into my woods by yourself, getting a half-hour head start. I will then go searching for you while you hide—for the next half-hour. If I find you, you will be mine to do with as I please."

Samantha shook on it and bid the sultan farewell for the night, and possibly always. Her inebriated spirits gave her enough courage to seal

the valediction with a kiss—the only one thus far—
letting his mouth taste what he might be missing
or gaining, after the morrow.

Early in the morning the next day, the sultan
stood proudly anchored to his horse. His six-foot
muscular form, dark hair, dashing looks and curled
mustache, exhibited more passion and persistence
than all the days where he only guessed at his op-
ponent's exuberance, without any formal proof.

Samantha also flaunted a matching self-
assuredness—because in her mind, she had convinced herself she was playing to win, either way.

The games began. Anything could happen.

The clock ticked away rapidly, to mark the end
of the hour which was to decide Samantha's fate.
She raced helplessly through trees and shrubs,
but the sultan caught her—five minutes before her
deadline.

Gracefully, he descended from his horse, looking as magnificent as Eros—the Greek god of love.
Taking her hand in his, he declared, "To do with
as I please. It pleases me to show you the extent of
my love by giving you the precious gift of freedom."

It was not an option Samantha had counted on.
Dumbfounded, she finally spoke, "I'm a fair player. I
will not back out on my part of the bargain, unless
of course you are nothing more than a lothario."

"Not in the least. I love you, Samantha. I
couldn't bear the thought of making you unhappy."

Being truly moved by the sultan's unselfish
love, Samantha embraced him—first affectionately,
then passionately—hoping to lead them to the inevitable.

Next, she lay in the grass and pulled the sultan
onto herself—ready for the promised consummation.
The feel of his bounteous arousal played havoc with

her senses. But the sultan pulled himself off her.

"Don't you desire me anymore?" she inquired.

The sultan slapped her hard, numbing her brain, and said, "You fool! Have you no idea what I feel for you? I couldn't possibly take you, knowing that you are with me purely out of obligation, just like all the other maidens of the harem—with your thoughts and heart belonging to someone else. I am a proud man. I will not be taken pity on, like a charity case."

"It is not pity, my lord. It is the creation of a beautiful memory we can cherish a lifetime, once we go our separate ways, to our very different worlds. We will never again have a chance to fulfill the wonderment of 'what if.' Let's just enjoy this moment given us. I assure you I come to you of my own free will."

Hearing her declaration, the sultan's strong mouth began exploring hers. His mind-drugging kisses awakened a frenzy of need so strong her legs went weak—buckling under with the anticipation of entering the world of the "never-never." Slowly and cautiously, the sultan undressed her, lingering on each part of her excited form, expertly teasing and releasing the tension from every aroused muscle. He talked about her caressing voice, enchanting eyes, soft shoulders, alluring breasts, smooth belly, splendid limbs, soft fragrant flesh and provocative slit—shaved for obvious Muslim appeal.

The sultan confessed that never before had he desired to taste a woman, but the arousal from the strongest of aphrodisiacs—love—made him crave participation in unmentionables. His goal was to let her sample a fire so great that she couldn't possibly walk away from him—for he feared the horror of letting go, after having had her.

As the sultan caressed Samantha's demanding flower, her body trembled involuntarily. Observing his effect on her, he continued titillating her, while grabbing her round derriere greedily to pull her closer to himself.

Samantha moaned, begging him to allow her body a feel of his. The sultan responded to her command like a love-slave, climbing up on top of her with the movements of a slithering cobra. His mouth lunged for hers, parting it with masculine arrogance, letting her taste her own nectar.

Samantha ripped off the pants that barely contained his cock, and received him into herself. Her dozens of muscles gripped to bring his one to full pleasure, squeezing out his hot lava. Marvelous feelings leaped out of their bodies—merging their souls and fusing their auras. Samantha could feel that together they had both come to life. The thought of inevitable separation made her fear the opposite.

As she lay securely in his arms, Samantha thought about what an indisputably fine man the sultan really was—unlike her preconceived notions. She began fearing the festering emotions that brewed dangerously within her, signaling the formation of a strong bond with him.

The dreadful moment for her to leave was at hand. She had to go, before she couldn't anymore. A black cloud of ghastly dilemma draped across her world. Her heart began to cry. The skies protested along with her—displaying nature's angry fireworks through thunder and lightning.

Grieving, Samantha rose up to a seated position, in preparation for her exit. But her eyes did not find grass or jungles about her—for she lay in her bed, next to a sleeping sultan, unsure of what had transpired. Was it a dream? Was it reality?

What was he doing there? Had they participated in defying gestures, or was he just feeling the warmth of her body next to his, on their possibly last night together? Samantha knew not what had taken place. Perhaps it was best left that way.

CHAPTER SEVENTEEN

The race that Samantha thought she had already run and concluded lay ahead of her—much like an unwritten exam after a night of grappling through it. The possibilities of its outcome both terrified and exhilarated her. As for what might have already taken place through the night, with the sultan sharing her bed, she didn't dare question or speculate.

Samantha slowly pulled herself out of her opulent bed, squirming her way around the sleeping sultan. But the brush of her arm sneaking by woke him. Taking her forearm in his hand, he ran his nose across its length, inhaling it like a sweet-smelling flower.

"Deserting me already, after the most memorable night of my life?"

"Whatever do you mean, my lord?"

With disappointment drooping his face, the sultan solemnly inquired, "Surely you haven't forgotten, have you?" Looking at Sam's blank expression, he began recapping the events—supposedly to refresh her memory.

"We agreed to approach our situation like two nobleman. Knowing you could never be happy with me, unless you go back to your life and resolve everything first, I offered you freedom—without the race. You in turn wanted to give yourself to me, not just to show gratitude, but so you may choose wisely between what you were leaving behind and what you were walking toward."

Hearing his account, Samantha became even more puzzled than before. She wondered why she had blocked out the incident so completely—especially if she was supposed to be saving it as a distinctive memory in her mind's reference library.

The sultan observed her expression, and commented, "You do remember, I hope. Say something, please. Your silence disturbs me."

Not wishing to confirm or deny, Samantha changed the topic and blurted out, "What happens now, my lord?"

"As soon as you are dressed, I will personally drive you wherever your heart desires. Then, after entrusting you to the care of your unworthy lover, I will walk away from you—temporarily. But I will return once again, after the moon completes another cycle—in twenty-eight days. At that time, you will have a choice to make. Come back to your lord and husband forever, no questions asked—or be prepared to be divorced by him, giving up all future claims to being his wife."

"Sounds more than fair, my lord... Let the record show that no matter what I choose, I will always think of you as a dear friend, fair lord, perfect love and gentle lover."

The sultan let out hearty laughter and said, "Gentle? Either you have a great sense of humor, or you've *completely* forgotten *everything*—because what we shared was anything but gentle.

A content smile took over the regal face as he played with his mustache and started to reminisce. "It was wild, reckless and unrestrained—much like a scuffle between two untamed beasts, expressing savage passion."

Samantha was quite taken aback by her recollection of the spellbinding night versus the sultan's. Could it be, she wondered, that the sultan was also prey to nothing more than a wanton dream? If that were the case, the relationship was still unconsummated, and officially, she had neither earned nor settled the right to her freedom.

Dare she ask her lord for details—to test if they were in harmony—or dare she just grab her chance to escape while she could? Could she really escape—since the walls that imprisoned her now were psychological, and would follow her wherever she went.

With an undercurrent of apprehension, Samantha burst out, "If it pleases my lord, I would like to hear his account of our bewitching night together—to take with me a memory of that which is most appealing to him."

The sultan pulled Samantha back into bed and drew her close to himself, wrapping his arms around her. His intense stare bore into her. "You really don't remember anything, do you?"

"My memory of the night feels like a dream—a perfect experience. I am not certain how much of it is reality and how much a creation of my mind."

"Very well then, why don't we just remember it as it pleased us individually. After all, a perfect memory is the best one can hope for—since it lasts long after the deed."

"But don't you want to know if it really happened?"

"All that matters is that Allah has granted us the memory and the experience as if it really happened, right here," he said, pointing to his heart, "where it matters the most."

Samantha's eyes moistened at his touching statement—her memory was engraved in his heart, not his head. She agonized, not knowing what to do.

Showing sensitivity to her dilemma, the sultan responded, "You still have twenty-eight days to change your mind and return to me, if you choose. But I insist that you leave now, and sort out your feelings. Because if you return, it must be without reservation. I refuse to share you with another man—mind, body or soul—just as I give you my word that I will belong exclusively to you and you alone."

"What about all the ladies in the harem?"

"They will be just like family, taking refuge in my home, but my body and soul will belong only to you."

Samantha embraced the sultan with all her might and declared, "For as long as I live, I will be grateful for having fainted at the mosque, all those weeks ago. I would have never met you otherwise."

"I, too, will always be grateful for you white folk not being able to handle the heatwave very well. For that is how I met you and another dear friend. He, too, was knocked out by the spell of the sun's hot fire."

"Your dear friend is also a foreigner?"

"Yes. I guess I feel comfortable with outlanders, due to a lack of obligation to proper protocol and decorum that keep me from being myself. Both yourself and Norman proved that."

With shock and surprise taking over her voice, Samantha sat up and shouted, "Norman? Not Norman Fairchild?"

"Why? Is he a sought-after convict?"

"No, nothing like that. But if you speak of Norman Fairchild from Queens, Canada, we need to talk."

The sultan smiled in amusement. "Is this where I'm supposed to suggest the proverbial 'small world'?"

"So, it *was* the Norman Fairchild I'm referring to."

The sultan sat up, with feet firmly grounded on the floor, nodded an affirmation, and added, "But don't expect me to turn against my friend in any way. I will not be disloyal—even for you."

"I would never ask that of you, my lord. But with your help, I may be able to put an end to the quest that brought me here in the first place."

"Thank Allah for such a pilgrimage. But why should I help end it if it will take you away from me?"

"Because it is more noble and vital than the love between a man and a woman."

"I shall reserve my promise to help until *after* I've heard your request."

What was shared next was up to Samantha. The wise words of the elderly harem begum—advising of the power she could have over the sultan—rang through her head repeatedly, like a loud echo. She had to play her cards to win. The ultimate noble goal that had been temporarily put to rest depended upon it.

Samantha made herself comfortable on a cushion, resting on the floor right at the sultan's feet. She then took his hands into hers and kissed them lovingly, while her eyes played their part in flirtatiously hypnotizing him for his full support. Knowing that she had him in the palm of her hand, she began squeezing tenderly for information.

Samantha's velvety smooth words finally made their way out of her calculating mouth. "Did Norman share the reason for his voyage with you?"

"Not really. But one thing was for certain. Norman wanted to learn everything about immortal things—from love, romance and sensuality, all the way to the ancient art and architecture they inspired."

"That sounds like the right Norman, all right—definitely not an impostor."

"Before I continue, I need to know what capacity you knew him in?"

"He was my brother's dearest friend, and my husband, until someone claimed his life—both their lives actually."

The sultan's eyes filled with tears, leaving the rest of him paralyzed. Samantha could see he was vulnerable despite what one might have expected of his training. Tenderly, she reached up her hand to his face, to wipe off his tears. The sultan remained still, trying to compose himself—without words, sighs or gestures.

His strong, somber voice finally emerged. "Who did this?"

"That is what I'm trying to find out, along with rectifying an error Norman's passion had executed."

"Norman never burdened me with what was on his mind, as much as it bothered me. For some reason, he felt it could hurt me. So we talked about everything else under the sun, while enjoying each other's gamesmanship."

"What sorts of games did you two participate in?"

"Polo, chess, badminton, riding, checkers, and Norman's favorite—treasure hunts."

"Tell me more about the treasure hunts."

"There really isn't that much to tell, other than his passion for making the clues progressively harder."

Samantha nodded in agreement.

The sultan looked at her gesture and commented, "I can see he liked playing that game with you also."

"No, not really. But as unintentional as it was, his last escapade has put my life in jeopardy."

"Perhaps he didn't realize what he was doing. It wouldn't be the first time."

"What do you mean, my lord?"

"The last treasure hunt he planned before leaving here was for parties unknown, with a treasure he didn't yet have in his possession."

Samantha muttered to herself, "That's the one."

"Did he ever get his hands on the treasure before leaving Kashmir?"

"I think not. From what I recall, he was hoping to secure its ownership in New Delhi."

Samantha became certain that the final resting place of the signet ring was New Delhi. Norman didn't have the luxury of time to hide it elsewhere before his hurried escape to Queens, via Calcutta. She thought to herself that the prolonged search was strictly designed to buy Norman time, since the treasure was hidden right near where it was to be started. But unfortunately, no one could bypass the trek across the country. There *was* no other way of accessing the clues that would lead to the end. Norman planned it that way.

Damn Norman!

CHAPTER EIGHTEEN

"Where are you taking me, my lord?"

"To your undeserving friend."

"How do you know *who* my friends are, or *where* they are, for that matter. It *has* been a month. They could be anywhere."

"Never underestimate the sultan. I'm a man of my word. When I promised you that I would take you back to them, I made a point of inquiring if anyone had been asking around for a beautiful foreign girl meeting your description in the appropriate time period. It wasn't hard to find them. They covered every single door in the business sector in your search, bi-weekly. At least, they seem to have come to their senses with respect to worrying about you—something they should have done all along, as gentlemen. In fact, it is their current behavior that allowed me to even *consider* returning you to them—dilemma or not."

"So where exactly are they staying?"

"I'm not sure. I just sent word that someone with information vital to locating you will be meeting them by the boardwalk near Dal Lake."

"So they're not even expecting to see me?"

"No, and It's him, not they. The foreigner has returned to New Delhi, convinced you must be long gone from Kashmir. He felt there wasn't much else that could be done here, since nothing had turned up in all this time. He decided to try his prospects in the capital city—the main consulate, for starters. And if that didn't work, he was planning on using some 'powerful' jewel for blackmailing two influential families into obtaining their help and cooperation."

"How did you find all this out, seeing that you haven't even met them?"

"The man who was to get in touch with them on my behalf told one of my servants that he had overheard a conversation to that effect—between your two friends. Nosy little breed, aren't they?"

Having barely informed Samantha of the status quo, the sultan pulled up his Rolls Royce to the boulevard. Samantha recognized a familiar figure—small frame, handsome face, olive skin, crooked teeth, mustache, the works—pacing restlessly. Excitedly, she pointed to him.

"That's him, my lord! That's him."

Samantha was thrilled that Feroz had not given up on his search for her and had stayed behind—"just in case."

"Have you decided what you are going to tell him about the last month?"

"No, not yet. But please know that your fairness can never be forgotten. I will see to it that you are not punished in any way."

"I wasn't thinking about that. I'm not afraid of penance, nor am I about to apologize for wanting to be your lover and redeemer. I was referring to your feelings toward me. I sense they've changed, yet you seem to be afraid of disclosing them."

"Twenty-eight days, remember. I shan't say anything before then."

"Twenty-eight days it is—but not a minute more."

Samantha kissed the sultan good-bye, and insisted on handling Feroz alone—leaving the sultan out of it entirely. Begrudgingly he went along, making a point of impressing upon her that it went against every fiber in him.

As Samantha made a mad dash to be reunited with Feroz, her heart vaulted backward toward the exotic life driving away from her. It felt like she was leaping out of *Arabian Nights* into the here-

and-now, through some time warp.

Feroz turned around and saw her. Time stood still as he stared at her in shock and said, "I can't believe this! It's really you?"

Samantha embraced him, and said, "In the flesh.

Feroz grabbed her shoulders, and said, "When I heard we might have a lead, not once did I suspect it meant you. I..."

Samantha could see that his emotional state had drained his vocal cords of their blood, rendering him speechless. Following a brief period of hyperventilating and steadying himself, Feroz finally came around. Facing east—with arms up in the air—he blurted out, "Thank you, Allah, for returning her to me. I will never let her out of my sight again."

Next, he turned to Samantha. "Tell me everything."

It was a question Samantha had both expected and dreaded. And now, here it was. Prudently, she said, "I can't talk about it. I'd rather you just fill me in on what's been happening at your end."

Feroz enveloped her in the protection of his arms and said, "I'm sorry. That was very insensitive of me. You must have survived *some* ordeal— and here I am, asking you to relive it. Forgive me, please. I'm just glad you have been returned— unharmed, I hope." Feroz paused briefly and looked up at her—as if seeking validation on his last comment—and then continued, "As far as I'm concerned, you needn't tell me anything. Just save it for the police."

"Please...*no* constabulary...*no* questions...*no* implications."

Feroz looked very perplexed, but restrained himself from pursuing it further. Samantha guessed it had to do with his belief that she didn't want to relive a horrible ordeal. Despite his erroneous driving force, she was just relieved that he didn't press her. If only she could hope for a similar response from Jake... But no, Jake was another story—beginning, middle and end—with doubts and innuendoes galore.

Feroz broke Sam's distant gaze by supportively explaining Jake's whereabouts, without once underrating his judgment call. It was obvious that he wasn't interested in winning her over that way.

Arm in arm, Samantha and Feroz walked over to the houseboat he was staying in. It was a smaller version of their previous three-bedroom giant. Feroz explained that Jake and he had thought better of their needs and traded down, since they hardly ever spent any time in it—not to mention the constant reminders from the extra empty room.

As Feroz took Samantha's hand and helped her aboard, her mind wandered to being helped onto the elephant saddle. It bothered her to realize that her thoughts were still in the sultan's captivity. She shook her head to rid her brain of him.

Feroz observed her agonizing expression and was baffled by it. It contradicted her otherwise well-tended face. In contrast, his own face looked spent—with dark bags beneath the eyes—but his expression was that of relief and unmatched ebullience.

As they sat down to tea, the air felt thick and tight with tension. Silence gripped them both, neither knowing quite where to begin. A lot of ground had to be covered, but not at the expense of cutting through taboo topics.

Samantha finally sliced through the choking air that was pushing them apart and said, "Whatever happened is over and done with. We need to pick up the pieces and move on. So, will you *please* start filling me in?"

"Of course, Sammy."

Having promised that, Feroz realized it was easier said than done, with the future hinging on the past as its foundation. Cautiously, he organized his thoughts, while his forefingers nervously worked away at his mustache.

"Our search was temporarily put on hold because of the more pressing issues. But I did manage to discern the location of our next clue before your disappearance. It was to be my dessert to you guys at our lunch meeting."

Feroz could see Sammy's impatience. He knew that she was one to prefer hearing the news first, particulars afterward. Without further delay, he informed her that the next clue would be found in Agra.

"Details, Feroz—I want details."

"I found a heart engraved on one of the wooden pillars." Feroz paused and looked up to the heavens, "Allah, forgive Norman for marring religious property." Returning his gaze to Samantha, he continued. "In it, Norman and Shanti's names were engraved, along with the words, 'True love is always eternal, be it etched in wood or in marble.'"

Samantha nodded, "Meaning Agra's Taj Mahal—the marble wonder of the world created to proclaim immortal love. I think I already know the answer to this, but by any chance, did he specify more?"

"Unfortunately not, Samantha."

"In any case, should we not be heading out to Agra?"

"All in good time, my lady. But first, we wait for Jake."

"Can we not just meet up with him there? It would be pointless for him to come here, only to head right back."

"When I heard we might have our only lead in

locating you, I promptly notified Jake. He informed me that he was going to leave immediately for Kashmir. He should be here within the next few hours."

Samantha's face returned to its original state of turmoil. On the one hand, she was overjoyed at the thought of being reconciled with Jake. But on the other, her mind shuddered at the cold investigation and cruel distrust that were sure to torture her. She began trembling with the anticipation of the worst part of her ordeal yet. Did Jake really have the right to know everything? Samantha thought not since he himself had been quite cryptic about the details of his life, save that which she had witnessed with her own eyes.

Samantha stopped her introspection and looked straight at Feroz, to apologize for her detached state. To her surprise, she heard him whisper to himself, "Jake had better get here fast, before I lose control," as he gave her a once-over, and allowed his body a preoccupation with hers.

A messenger from the telegraph office delivered a note to Feroz, informing him that Jake would be delayed until the morning.

"Great! Just what I needed! Help me out of this one, Allah—before I do something I'll have to regret later," said Feroz, trepidation ravaging his body. He began pacing, wringing his hands and avoiding looking at Sam.

Blood rushed tingling warmth through Samantha as she stared at him with brazen ambivalence—recognizing his yearning for her. Feroz tried desperately to contact Jake—"to save him a trip." But Samantha knew there was more to it— his not wanting to be alone with her for the night, among other things.

To Feroz's dismay, Jake had already checked out of his Delhi address, to parts unknown.

Night fell. The elements stirred dismally. Splattering rain clouds drowned out the moonlight and the sounds that attested to life outside the houseboat. Samantha and Feroz felt truly marooned.

Feroz paced back and forth in the sitting area, repeatedly checking the windows to see if the storm was letting up—despite the obvious sounds and movements that shook their boat.

"Would you like me to round you up a dove to check the water level outside?" Samantha teased, hoping to relax Feroz.

"What?"

"Never mind," said Sam, appreciating the difference in their habituation.

Never before had she seen him so uncomfortable at the mere thought of being alone with her. Judging by the way he was avoiding her, she gathered he wanted her and was fighting desire.

Samantha's own high emotions intensified the delicious situation. She walked over to where he was, embraced him, and said, "Don't be so afraid. We're both mature adults. I know we will never let anything get out of hand that wasn't within mutually comfortable limits."

Feroz responded with a sigh of relief—letting out all the pressures that had built up within his body—and wrapped his arms around her, while his face nuzzled into her neck. Samantha kissed his forehead. Instantly, his eyes made contact with hers, seeking permission to taste her mouth. After a prolonged deliberation, she brought her closed lips to his, and inhaled the moist breath that emerged from his core. Its intense heat told her of the fires that were burning within. But she didn't dare part her lips to allow his flesh to enter hers.

Next, Samantha led him to his bed and persisted in drawing out his desire. Slowly, she began stroking his clothed body with her feathery touch—teaching him about timelessness. She played his back like a harp and his groin like a flute, creating an enchanting melody for his senses. She could see that his body ached as she deliberately varied the pressure and duration of each caress. But he didn't dare push or withdraw.

Embarrassed, Feroz admitted, "You must think I'm an inexperienced fool—getting so turned on by such benign gesturing. But it's a combination of a lot of different things—the suspense of 'whether or not,' for one. I can even honestly say that it is more torturous than the thought of not having you."

Sam knew that the stiffness in Feroz's pants cried for fulfillment, as did the cleavage between her own legs. But she opted for an unconventional intimacy. Like a graceful feline, her dressed body coiled around his—purring affectionately. The erotic dance lingered, until she witnessed his undulating body sigh, moan and groan with complete satisfaction—just as he had observed hers, the night she was reunited with Jake, in the Khan guest bedroom.

Truly, it was a dazzling experience neither had known before.

CHAPTER NINETEEN

The hot pink cap of the rising sun started to make its way up the horizon at Dal Lake. Rays beamed from it like outstretched limbs of a lazy yawn. Everything sparkled with dewy freshness after the night's rainfall. To each waking eye, the day promised to be warm, passive and uneventful. To Jake, it promised vitality, with the possibility of his recent turmoil turning around.

Walking up to the doorway of the houseboat, Jake felt anxious—not knowing what to expect. Due to the early hour, he unlocked the door himself and quietly slipped in, not wishing to disturb Feroz.

There she stood, making his head spin. Seeing her was a shock he hadn't quite anticipated. It brought back memories of the days when she was merely an illusion—not to be confused with reality. Samantha reached out her long arms to welcome him with a hug. Jarred by the facsimile, Jake started to step backward—eyes glassy with fear and disbelief.

"You look like you've just seen a ghost, Jake. You're not afraid of me, are you?"

One by one, a series of shiny beads gushed out of Jake's bleary eyes. "I thought I'd lost you for good! I didn't know if you were dead, alive, hurt, or had simply run away. Never before had I felt such emptiness and despair in my life, not even when..."

"What were you going to say, Jake?"

"It's not important. All that matters is that you're here. When I heard we might have a lead, I didn't for a minute think it could be you. I was even too afraid to get my hopes up for the slightest clue—not being able to face up to any more disappointment."

Jake squeezed Samantha so tight that she feared suffocation. His arms traveled up and down her body—as if taking inventory of his chattel. It felt great to be in his secure embrace once again. All doubts vanished. He *was* unquestionably her true love.

But then suddenly his body tensed, and his steely strong hands took charge of her shoulders—pushing her an arm's length away. "What happened?" he asked with a stern, interrogative expression.

Samantha pulled away voluntarily, before he would have a chance to force a greater distance between them. With downcast eyes, she responded, "I'd rather not talk about it."

Without once considering giving her the benefit of the doubt, his brows raised and his menace-laden voice hissed out accusations—tearing her to shreds—insinuating her involvement in criminal activity.

Was this the man she loved? One who could not empathize with her desire to put her ordeal behind her, just as Feroz had done? Or was he the cynic who was always too quick to judge her? What had made him that way, she wondered. Was it his surreptitious past, the painful incident he almost referred to moments ago, or the artist who had left behind the beautiful pieces in his apartment?

Samantha hadn't noticed that she had cupped her ears with her hands to block out Jake's rage until he pulled them off.

"Damn it, lady! You're going to listen, *and* you're going to talk. I've been wasting my life worrying about you, trying to rescue you, while you expect to waltz in here without an explanation! Sorry, lady, but no cigar."

Not knowing how to respond to the outrageous burst of venomous shouts and shakes, Samantha stood defenseless.

Hearing the commotion, Feroz woke up and came to them. Seeing Samantha jailed in a corner, with arms shielding her face from fear of possible blows, Feroz lost all self-control. With unsubdued rage, he thunderously shouted, "STOP INTIMIDATING HER! We can't begin to guess what she might have survived. And for what? You treating her like this?"

Feeling challenged, Jake's temper was further aggravated. He raised his arm and clenched his fist into an unmistakable weapon. Swiftly, Feroz intervened, swinging it right back into Jake's face, tearing through his upper lip. Blood gushed everywhere, staining everything within spurting vicinity.

Samantha had always stood up for herself, but mixed emotions had victimized her this time. Just this once, it felt good to have someone stand up for her, helping her through a vulnerable moment. The sultan would have probably intervened even faster, she thought.

What followed was disgraceful, since it involved two intelligent grown men not working together toward a noble goal. Blows, angry words—the works. To an outsider it would have looked like a drunken brawl.

The skirmish continued until Feroz was satisfied he had knocked all the steam and excess strength out of Jake—ensuring Samantha could no longer be exploited.

But as all noblemen's fights end with a handshake, this one also ended with a reaffirmation of friendship—right after Jake acknowledged that his hysterics might have been unjustified and that he owed Samantha a sincere apology. Shamefully, he turned toward where she was standing, only to discover she had left during the commotion.

Samantha walked the streets of Srinagar to

clear her head. She couldn't help but notice the contrasts about her—destitution versus riches, pain versus laughter, sweet smells versus pungent ones, and so on. They made her think about her own feast-or-famine love life—from loneliness and liability with Norman, to three equally impassioned suitors. Her choice was next to impossible! She enjoyed Jake's wit, intelligence, quirky charm and shared acculturation. But where his sense of trust stopped, Feroz's admirable loyalty and sensitivity took over. And then, there was the sultan—in a class all his own. No one could *dream* of possibly matching his courtship, passion, or power. But he was not one to be toyed with or kept waiting. Twenty-seven days—a decision had to be reached by then, treasure hunt or not. Dare she use her heart or her head, to make the most important decision of her life? One thing was for certain— she didn't appreciate having to rush love.

Despite her three admirers, Samantha sat alone in one of the boulevard cafes, staring aimlessly into the lotuses sprawled across the lake. She soothed the fire within her by sipping away on a cool, creamy mango shake. Everything was a blur to her teary eyes. The two figures who approached her table went unnoticed until they walked right up to her.

Samantha looked at the pathetic face that was hiding behind Feroz, seemingly to have him intervene on his behalf. Reluctantly she offered him a seat and said, "I prefer a man who pleads his own case—*after* a proper apology, of course."

Feroz took his cue and left them alone.

"Before you say anything, Jake, there are a few things I need to make clear to you. For starters, if we are to have any kind of a relationship, you can't be treating me like this. I have never

deliberately given you grounds for fraudulent suspicion. Yet, whenever in doubt, it's the only option
you choose to take. I'm sure your previous baggage has laden you with reasons, but I expect you
to treat me based on my own virtue."

Jake listened quietly, not having many alternatives. But he didn't look too pleased with what
he might have to open up to.

Looking at his unsure gaze, Samantha asked,
"Would you like me to continue, or would you prefer to leave now?"

As weary as Jake looked, he urged her to go on.

"Last, but not least, I expect you to have enough
respect for me to share your personal past with
me. I wouldn't ask it of you if it didn't affect us.
But since I've endured enough abuse because of
it, I insist you share it with me. Don't expect me to
understand you otherwise."

Jake squinted his eyes and threw back a big
sigh. Discontentedly, he endeavored to release the
words that seemed hidden in the dark recesses of
his brain.

"If you *must* know—I've been fooled, used and
abused by the one person I loved and trusted
enough to make a lifelong commitment to. *Now*,
can you understand why I will never again allow
myself to be in that position?"

"We've all been hurt like that at one time or
another, Jake. But it is important that we not be
consumed by it, recycling the pain endlessly. I can't
stop you from choosing that for yourself, but I, for
one, refuse to waste my life on it."

Samantha observed the hesitation on Jake's
face as he struggled to get his words out but
couldn't. She decided to end both the meeting and
the relationship, right then and there.

"Looks like we can't see eye to eye on this one,

Jake. Why don't we just call it a difference of opinion, and bid *adios*."

Jake recognized that she meant business. Normally, he would have never allowed himself to be railroaded into a conversation he wasn't completely ready for, but something within nudged him to talk, having already sampled her absence. He dove right into the deep end—leaving no room for a change of heart.

"I was married to a curator named Sharon. She was beautiful, talented, interesting, exciting and very independent. In fact, it was her independence that drew me to her in the first place. We were both comfortable with pursuing our own careers and interests, without dragging each other around. But then she became less and less available to me, being more and more driven by her profession. I could have even lived with that, if it weren't for the secrets and clandestine meetings she started keeping from me. When confronted, she refused to divulge anything, on the grounds of professional confidence. What possible secret could a curator have, that she couldn't share with her husband? I wondered. I began fearing her possible involvement in something illicit. She called me paranoid. The silly issue became the focus of a power struggle. Foolishly, we allowed our relationship to disintegrate over it. Separation became inevitable."

Jake paused to wipe his face, drenched with salty wetness from sweat and tears, anticipating the crescendo. The couple barely balanced themselves at the edge of their respective seats, awaiting...

Jake persevered. "One day, she insisted on speaking with me, urgently, back at the house. Sensing the despondency in her voice, I rushed right over. When I got there, she started off by be-

ing very friendly, presenting me with a peace offering—some strange pava shell chimes. I became
ecstatic, thinking that she was going to suggest
reconciliation. Boy, was I wrong! I realized that
when I found out she wasn't alone! The jock who
had accompanied her came out of the kitchen and
introduced himself as Swami—a supposed expert
on everything from health foods and meditation to
hypnosis. Sharon told me in no uncertain terms
that he was more her type, and that she wanted a
quick, amicable divorce to start her life over—with
him. Naturally, I was furious, since her agenda
was quite different from what I had in mind. Rage
overcame me. I found myself pounding out a total
stranger. Of course, that didn't last very long, since
the meathead was a lot stronger than me. I completely blacked out."

The story came to an abrupt end, with sirens
going off in Jake's head. The very suspicious nature that he was trying to circumvent returned
with a vengeance.

"Oh my gosh! That is when I first saw you,
before those dreams began! You are their accomplice! And to think that I had blocked out everything, all this time. What the hell is your game
anyway, lady?"

Shock and outrage heated Samantha's face
with a horrible sting. Anger burst throughout her
skull, blurring her vision with dark shadows. Had
he gone mad? she wondered. He made no sense
whatsoever. His faculties seemed impaired. What
was causing his preposterous behavior? One thing
was for certain, she wasn't interested in finding
out the extremes it could lead to. Quickly she
grabbed her purse and sprinted to where Feroz
sat, a few tables away. Grabbing his hand, she
pulled him to run with her.

Jake leered at her with eyes pink from wrath and shook his petulant head in disgust as he shouted, "Cat got your tongue? Can't say anything, can you? 'Cause you're guilty as sin, with no-o-o-o defense."

Seeing that she was long gone, he muttered to himself, "At least she didn't patronize me with untruths and concoctions."

CHAPTER TWENTY

Rage and shock overcame Feroz, doubts about Samantha not once entering the picture. She had told him so little, yet he blindly accepted her. His patience, trust and tenderness triumphed over her. If only she could feel for him the same love she had started to develop for Jake, everything would be perfect. But she knew that love is known to follow neither logic nor reason.

Samantha planned to head out to Agra as soon as possible. Although the mission didn't affect or excite Feroz, he insisted on escorting her. As for Jake, she wasn't certain whether or not he was still committed to their goal—or if he was in the country, for that matter.

As with New Delhi, Sammy was delirious about arriving in a city that boasted the finest architectural achievements of the Mogul era. Its eminence was just what she needed to take her mind off her problems. She was especially excited about setting foot in the world-famous mausoleum—the Taj Mahal—created flawlessly by Shah Jahan to immortalize his love for his beautiful wife, Mumtaz Mahal.

Feroz checked them into two adjoining rooms with a regal connecting parlor at the luxurious Taj-View Hotel. Its grandeur tried to mimic the style in the sultan's harem, but fell short. But to the majority who had never experienced such worldly delights, Taj-View was an exquisite palace—from traditional furniture and Persian carpets all the way to intricate artifacts and cushions.

As the twosome tried to relax and recoup from their tedious journey, Samantha began reading up on the divine monument that had no rival. Her heart was always partial to the intersections where art and history met. Amour made it all the more delightful.

Sammy read about the matchless beauty of the seventeenth century testimonial. It was described as having a sculpturesque quality, created by the most outstanding talent and laborers, involving twenty-two years, over twenty thousand pairs of hands, and an unrestrained flow of imperial treasures. Luminous white marble and sandstone boasted intricate inlays of precious and semiprecious stones. Several dozen gems were used in any given flower to achieve the desired shades of color.

Feroz watched Sam's enthusiasm and suggested they take an after-dinner stroll through the supreme magic of the Taj—seeing that it had already captivated her.

Nothing in Samantha's extraordinary imagination came close to the overpowering and breathtaking impression that stunned her. She was paralyzed by the sublime structure. It went from a sensuous creature dancing against the fiery orange curtain of sunset to a haunting ethereal jewel in the silvery moonlight. If there ever was an inanimate object with a breathing soul, this was it, Samantha thought. Its lifelike presence led her to think that it might actually speak to her—telling her where Norman's next clue was taking refuge. She quivered, thinking how she might find it otherwise.

Next, Feroz took Samantha to the banks of the adjoining river, Yamuna. Tides embraced the shore, bathing it with powerful sprays. Samantha watched the moon change the sparkling waves to a bounteous supply of milk. Her heart began to race, remembering the time that Feroz walked her to the waters of the Ganges, participating in her erotic dream.

The ambiance of the enchanting night was perfect for a whimsical liaison. It personified romance and seduction. But Feroz didn't dare take advantage of it. His courtesies extended to the hotel—with him offering to retire to his room, leaving Samantha the luxury of relaxing in privacy.

Seven days went by. Samantha and Feroz faithfully spent all their waking hours going over the majestic structure with a fine-tooth comb. But fate was not on their side, for they came out empty-handed each time. Then, just as they had almost given up on the eve of the eighth day, a familiar silhouette approached them. But since the blazing red ball of sun was behind him, they were unable to identify his visage. His apparel—an embroidered *pajama kurta* and Kolapuri leather sandals—made him look like a tour guide in keeping with the ambiance, or a tourist who was getting right into it. Feroz guessed that it was the latter. Sure enough, it was Jake, yielding to the arresting culture.

With each approaching step of his sandals, Samantha's guts wrenched tighter and tighter. Her mind could hold but one thought: the chameleon-like mental metamorphosis that her Dr. Jekyll/Mr. Hyde could snap in and out of. She knew that she wasn't ready for another confrontation. Hurriedly, she grabbed Feroz by the arm and said, "Let's go."

Feroz obliged. Jake followed faithfully behind. As they reached the formidable gate, Samantha felt the chase couldn't possibly endure any longer. She gathered enough courage to face the unscrupulous Jake Alexander, and turned around.

"What exactly do you want from me? I didn't think there was an accusation *left* in the universe that you hadn't already discharged at me."

Shamefully, Jake replied, "I know I have no right to ask you to listen to me of my own merit, but please indulge me for the sake of our principal goal."

"Very well. But you have only five minutes to voice what you have to say, from a safe distance, at least five feet away."

Jake bowed his head, with hands folded like a *namaste*, acknowledging her request.

"A grave mistake was made on my part. I realize that now, having come up with a theory that pieces together our messy puzzle into a clear picture. It absolves you of all the misplaced blame I hurt you with."

"Thank goodness for that," Samantha said sarcastically.

"I don't blame you for being upset, but please hear me out."

Samantha looked at her watch and said, "Four minutes and counting down."

"My ex-wife, Sharon, was always looking for rare pieces that would ennoble her as a curator. Somehow, she must have found out about the priceless signet ring that Norman could get his hands on. Knowing Sharon, I'm almost certain she must have accosted him and tried to get him to sell it to her. Norman obviously refused. But since Sharon had always been one to get what she wanted, no matter who got hurt, she must have come up with an alternative plan, with you and myself as pawns. I feel we were set up from the very start—right from the time when she enraged me into the physical fight with her hypnotist friend. I have a strong hunch he used his skill to manipulate my mind into falling in love with you— probably with the aid of one of your pictures and those bloody chimes. I knew I should have thrown out the damn things right when she gave them to me. But the fool that I was, I gave them a prime place in my bedroom, to remind me of her vices—using something she knew I'd like, as a way of warming up to me."

Jake seemed to realize that he was getting emotional and sidetracked. One look at Sam's impatiently tapping foot and he was back on track again. "Sorry about getting carried away like that. More to the point—do you have a picture of yourself in a revealing dress, with outstretched arms?"

"Not that I see the relevance, but yes. Norman painted his rendition of me as Aphrodite—the Greek goddess of love—depicted as you've described. Don't ask me to show it to you, though. It was stolen from Norman's nightstand at the hospital."

"Bingo! That proves my point! For months before I actually met you, I had compelling dreams about you—always in that form... Don't you see? I was set up to fall for you! Subsequently, we were both set up to flee Queens, in a desperate hunt for the signet ring. Sharon knew my weakness for adventure, especially with someone like you. She used it to further her cause. It all makes sense—the dreams, the tabloids, Norman's murder, Robin Hutton's homicide—everything. She was so good at setting us up that even you and I ended up mistrusting each other."

Reluctantly, Samantha was also beginning to see the picture. She remembered how some curator had harassed Norman when she herself had been left out of the details. As well, she recalled that Jake had insisted on having seen her somewhere before when they first ran into each other. At the time she had dismissed it as a trite line, but he was possibly telling the truth all along—knowing the blunt person he was. And then there was the missing painting. But despite the facts that were falling into place, there were still several unanswered questions.

"Jake, if it was Sharon all along, how would you explain the car accident aimed at Norman, or the whole ordeal with the Ranas and the Choudhrys, for that matter?"

"The car accident I'm not sure about. It could have been a mere coincidence or unfinished revenge. As for the two dynasties, we may very well have opened Pandora's box *after* our arrival here. Then again, any one of these people, or a separate party altogether, could have been working with my greedy ex-wife all along. After all, she had to have found out about the ring somehow."

Despite the confusion and fear that smothered Samantha, she was relieved that Jake wasn't crazy after all. She wondered if he was still in love with her, seeing that he had labeled it as nothing more than a set-up. In any case, she was relieved at being cleared of his false criminal charges against her. But at the same time, it petrified her to think of his permanent emotional scars, inflicted by such a nefarious individual as Sharon. Surely they would always haunt him.

Samantha snapped herself out of her deliberations and said, "Now that we've uncovered the mystery, can we pack it in, turn it over to the police, and return home?"

"No, Samantha, the mystery has just become bigger than ever. And although it might have become clearer, it's a far cry from being solved. What's more, our current knowledge is even more dangerous to us than before. But we can't very well go to the police without substantiated evidence. No, Sammy, our problems have become worse than ever—or at least our recognition of them anyway.

It isn't just a matter of restoring the royal contract by handing over the signet ring anymore. Now we also have to worry about Sharon and lord knows who else as wild cards."

"Could you not give the falcon to Sharon, instead of the ring—to get her off our backs? It's market value has to be significantly more."

"That might be foolish, because we would be admitting to our current knowledge and fears. Besides, we have no guarantees that it will stop there. For all we know, she could still come after us for the signet ring we've promised to some other deadly folk. For now, it's best if we simply play dumb."

Feroz interjected, "I suggest you two take your private conversation elsewhere. In a case of such magnitude, even the trees have ears."

Samantha and Jake concurred. The threesome loaded up into a taxi, shut their mouths, and headed back to the Taj-View.

Back at the suite, the little team indulged in a customary evening tea—designed for the purposes of unwinding, taking stock of the day, and organizing the morrow.

Having their emotions in check once again, they decided to recap everything that had happened thus far, with or without their knowledge. Clear patterns evolved on both counts.

As they scrutinized the treasure hunt, it was obvious that Norman had planted clues in various points of interest to him, separated by enough distance to allow himself and Shanti ample time to escape. The only consistency was that all clues were born by phallic symbols of one sort or another—poles, pillars, erotic sculptures.

Samantha suddenly jumped to her feet with the same enthusiasm she had shown each time she deciphered a clue.

"I have it! Norman must have seen the four poles that surround the Taj as four phalluses—in competition for the one object of desire. It has to be one of them. And I'd even be willing to bet that it's the northern one—in keeping with the north pillar at the mission church, where the hunt first started."

"Sheer genius, Sammy!"

The sensual dancing queen of the sunset and the ethereal jewel of the moonlight transformed yet again—to a virginal maiden—at dawn. The northern pillar looked more magnificent than ever: tall, firm, radiant and unblemished, with a moist sheen from the kiss of fog.

Three pairs of hands stroked its hard wet surface, probing it as if it were Braille. The marble phallus relented, surrendering its exposed information—a concentric circle pattern that mimicked the artistry of New Delhi's Connaught Place. It displayed faint etched-in coordinates that could easily have been overlooked as cracks or lines of erosion—unless, of course, they represented life lines.

CHAPTER TWENTY-ONE

The sun rose to its peak, bringing with it a glare that reflected blindingly off the white marble. Samantha wondered if they were rays of hope or flames of destruction that breathed down so intensely.

Having located the potent information, the crew wanted to say good-bye to the laudable structure that still echoed its former glory and splendor. But Samantha didn't dare part before paying homage to the immortal lovers. To her disappointment, the dome only held their cenotaphs, with the actual graves residing elsewhere. *Why is everything so intangible and concealed?* she wondered. Dismayed, she suggested they move on.

Another race was planned—this time to the concentric circles of Connaught Place, New Delhi.

The short voyage ended at the Marina Hotel—embedded right in the Connaught mandala. Its location was almost custom-tailored to meet the crew's needs—with its proximity to the infamous coordinates, shops, restaurants, transportation and the tranquil central park. Finally, everything appeared to be falling into place—simplistically, or so it seemed.

A closer analysis of the coordinates revealed why Norman's latest clue had been so straightforward. As one might have expected, he selected the most mind-boggling labyrinth of alleyways, congestion and confusion, leading to hundreds of viable options, with not one standing out above the rest. A matter of hours was certain to stretch out to a matter of days, possibly weeks. Hopelessness enveloped them once again. Feroz had to remind them of the erudite guru's words, to afford impetus.

Back to the drawing board had become a rule rather than an exception. This time, the threesome shifted focus to possible accomplices.

Samantha turned to Jake and pleaded, "Being Sharon's ex-husband and an expert at theory formulation, I hope you can enlighten us on *how* she accessed the classified information on Norman and the ring. It might help us with our stalemate, especially if it can highlight a conspirator out here."

"We haven't the time to waste on speculation. Can't you just approach Sharon candidly, 'for old times sake,' and strike up a bargain with her—pleading for her help in exchange for the falcon?" Feroz interjected.

"No, my friend. Like I said before, *that* could be lethal. Sammy, can you not think of anyone who Norman might have shared the information with?"

"Norman didn't know anyone in Queens other than Allen and me. The information must have leaked out here in India."

"But Sharon never came here, and as far as I know, she had no connections in India. But then again, there is a lot I don't know about my ex-wife," Jake said, shaking his head in frustration .

Jake reverted back to deep thought. He appeared to be fighting the demons that obstructed his thinking. Then, suddenly, with chin grasped in hand, he inquired, "Could *Allen* possibly have known Sharon and divulged the information to her?"

Samantha reached into her purse, pulled out Allen's last picture, and showed it to Jake. "Here, take a look at this. The woman with him is someone he had an affair with before the accident claimed his life. And as far as I know, she was the only woman he would have been intimate with after having learned all about Norman's true identity, plans and possessions. Could she possibly be a friend of Sharon's who could have passed on the information to her? Because knowing Allen, he wouldn't share a confidence like that with just anyone."

Rage flooded from Jake. Every blood vessel in his face pumped to capacity as he clenched and crumpled the picture. "Why, that bitch!"

"I was right! She is one of Sharon's friends, isn't she?"

Thunderously, Jake shouted, "*No*, nothing like that."

"I don't get it. You seemed to have recognized the face in the picture—un...unless, it is Sharon herself."

"What I don't understand is, how the hell did she smoke him out?" shouted Jake.

"According to Allen, he met her at an East Indian art auction in Queens. From what I recall, they seemed to have hit it off right from the start. He was amazed at how a fascinating and knowledgeable lady like her seemed interested only in his experiences, without once talking about herself."

Jake interrupted. "I'll just bet..."

With horror on her face, Samantha declared, "Oh my gosh, Jake. I just remembered Norman mentioning a terrible disagreement between himself and Allen, just before the car crash. Could it be that he was trying to convince Norman to sell? I wonder if it was the altercation that inadvertently caused the collision?"

"Knowing Sharon, I'm sure even that didn't stop her, because obviously she started to harass Norman directly. And to think I was actually married to that bitch, sharing my bed with her! Never again will I allow a woman to fool me like that," Jake said hatefully.

There it was again—the raw wound, lashing

out in mistrust. Samantha wondered if it would ever heal, or if the scar would be a callused version of what she had already been experiencing.

Although Samantha and Jake were silent in their contemplations, body language expressed their disquiet loud and clear. Fortunately, Feroz cut in.

"We haven't the time to brood and bicker. We'll lose all perspective if we do. Sharon certainly didn't treat the issue personally; neither can we afford to. If we are to be a good match for her schemes, we need to be just as proficient as she—without emotions obscuring our thinking."

Samantha was surprised that Feroz was always the one to move things along, even though it had nothing to do with him. Although she didn't quite understand his motivation, she was grateful for it, since she, too, wanted to wrap things up as quickly as possible. She had major decisions to make in her private life.

Since a local accomplice seemed unlikely, the threesome went back to their blind search. The area near the coordinates was scanned thoroughly—up, down and around—several times over, but to no avail. Whether it was the actual ring or a clue bringing them a step closer to it, the congested concentric bowels continued to conceal it. An entire week deteriorated in the futile inspection.

Personally, Jake continued to maintain a safe distance between himself and Sammy—though a part of him still appeared to desire her, in light of his discussion with her. Jake had told Sam that he needed to sort out the confusion in his mind about his feelings for her. He feared that as strong as the bond between them was, it might just be a product of brainwashing. And if that was the case, he was bound to end up hurting them both once he realized the limitations to the depth of his emotions. He had thereby decided to take his time in making the appropriate decisions. But time was not a luxury that Samantha could afford. With sixteen days already gone, only twelve more remained before she had to give an answer to the spellbinding creature who invaded her each and every thought.

Looking at the disturbed expression on Sam's face, Feroz said, "Since I don't seem to be doing much good here, I might as well take a break and tend to some of the things that I have been neglecting in my own business."

"Certainly," Sammy and Jake blurted out in unison.

Samantha threw her arms around Feroz affectionately and said, "I can't begin to thank you enough for your loyal friendship. Never in my life have I seen anything like it. You've put everything in your life on hold for us. I hope it hasn't jeopardized your business, or put you in an awkward position with your family—seeing that you are taking residence with us here, with your house just a few miles away. I know you would have preferred us staying in the luxury of your lovely home, but it was important that we reside in this location, with complete privacy and without involving your innocent mother and sisters."

Samantha stopped her courteous speech, since she noticed Feroz pulling away from her and her monologue, eager to get on with his agenda. Without further delay, she concluded, "I won't keep you any longer. But please, *do* keep in touch...and return to us as soon as possible."

Feroz nodded, pulled away, shook hands with Jake and made his way out with his garment bag.

An uneasiness overcame Samantha. She had enjoyed Feroz's companionship and the warmth he brought to the progressively freezing relationship between herself and Jake. Surely, she would miss him.

Following Feroz's hasty exit, Samantha and Jake stood alone, face to face, for the first time since the outbreak of emotion. At last, they could no longer avoid fathoming the extent of tension that had evolved between them.

Samantha broke the unwieldy silence with, "Now what?"

Jake shrugged his shoulders and said, "Don't look at me. I've got enough problems of my own."

Listlessly, Samantha inquired, "Would I be helping those problems if I moved to another hotel—or Feroz's home, perhaps?"

"No, I don't think that would be necessary—though I'm not certain of anything anymore," Jake replied reluctantly. "Very well, then. I'll stay here for now. But do let me know if you require a change in the status quo of our living arrangements."

As much as Samantha appreciated Jake's pain and ambivalence, she was disturbed by his attitude toward her.

Despite their truce, the couple continued maintaining an awkward distance—burying themselves in their project notes for the remainder of the evening.

Samantha utilized her time in formulating a chronological account of events. She felt recapping might lend itself to a desperately needed new stratagem.

The account began with the birth of an illegitimate first-born in a royal family with an infertile *begum.* With fresh tears to her womb, the ousted mother committed suicide, having hurriedly secured parents and parentage for her denied infant. Fifteen years later, by fluke or fate, the barren woman herself eventually bore fruit—giving the royal family one final chance at self-preservation. Next, the actual firstborn discovered his true identity and the tragic circumstances that surrounded it. Being devastated, he was overcome with but one desire—to avenge the death of his biological mother, who had been sacrificed brutally to pride. The fires of vengeance and bitter envy were further fueled when the lords of justice threw in love as a wild card. Like a madman lost to reason, Norman masterminded the disappearance of the very emblems the egotistic dynasty would have killed for. The only way they could be recovered was through an ingenious chase to end all chases, weaving through symbols of life's greatest gifts—love, passion, faith, and immortality—teaching a "priceless lesson."

The more Samantha thought about it, the more she realized that the end had to do with humiliating the creed that valued pride over human life. Unfortunately, however, Norman lost his own life before the edification. Observing the prodigious intricacies, Sam wondered, could Norman *really* have left any of the details to fate alone, knowing his life was in danger? It didn't appear so.

With notes in arms and Norman's driving forces in mind, Sam fell asleep. Images of a distraught young woman with fresh wounds in her womb repeatedly ran through her mind. Not a single dream escaped the pain with which she must have dragged herself to the mission and the pontoon bridge she eventually jumped off.

"The pontoon bridge! That's it," Samantha mumbled.

Reluctantly, she walked over to the wing chair Jake was taking refuge in and shook him to complete alertness. "I have it, Jake—that is, if you're still interested."

"Interested in what?"

"The signet ring."

"Of course! Why else would I still be sticking around?"

Obviously, he was trying to make a point with respect to his feelings toward her, or lack thereof. But inasmuch as it seared her heart, Samantha soared above it and announced, "The pontoon bridge, right here in Connaught Place."

"Do go on."

"Norman's driving force was avenging his mother's suicide—executed on the very bridge we've walked hundreds of times, scanning our coordinates. I'm almost certain that he hid the Rajput pride and joy in the soil Kamani jumped into. I'll bet you my last rupee that I'm right. Come, let's go claim it so we can put an end to everything, and get on with our lives."

"Are you crazy? We're not going anywhere at this hour! We'll have better luck tomorrow morning."

Whether it was fear of everything coming to an end, the dark, or something entirely different, Jake showed excellent salesmanship in convincing Samantha to hold off until the morning. But he failed to provide comfort to her tossing and turning body, with guts being whipped by nervousness.

CHAPTER TWENTY-TWO

Fear, excitement and lack of restful sleep nauseated Samantha. The hour had come when she would unravel the final step of her search.

Samantha decided to give Feroz a call, since he had been a faithful accomplice all along—despite a lack of personal gain. But to her surprise, he wasn't home—and hadn't been for several weeks. According to his very upset mother, he was still supposed to be with her and Jake. Samantha's heart sank with worry. She was certain he had been hurt in connection with his innocent involvement with them. Without any delay or contemplation, she rushed out to the living room of her suite, calling out desperately for Jake. She wanted to get to the bottom of Feroz's disappearance, placing the signet ring on the back burner once again.

But to her shock, Jake was gone. Gone were his possessions, and gone was the falcon—the only tangible bargaining chip that could have bought protection for them. Samantha was stunned and baffled at the turn of events, because this time the complication was undoubtedly not something Norman had planted—so close to unraveling the mystery.

Terror gouged away cruelly at all of Samantha's faculties. She was more confused than ever before. Did Jake leave in the middle of the night for emotional or materialistic reasons? It certainly appeared to be the latter, since he now had both the priceless tokens, in a matter of speaking—with the falcon already in his possession and the signet ring only a short walk away. Samantha shuddered to think what it all meant. His constant mistrust in her vouched for his own unscrupulous-

you were planning on beating me to the ring and stealing the falcon as a bonus."

"You never give up, do you? How *dare* you think you can accuse me like that, to establish your own innocence?"

"Evidently, neither one of us seems to know the half of it, with both of us censuring each other. But get this—would I still be standing here if I had any idea what was going on?"

Reluctantly, Jake confessed, "I guess not."

"Was the Choudhry goon still following you around when this happened, Jake?"

"As far as I know, they took him off our case a while back—seeing that we weren't turning up anything and no contacts had been made with the Ranas."

"Then who else could it be?"

"Who else but Mr. Feroz Chanan Khan?"

"You don't really believe that, do you, Jake?"

"It all makes sense. First, he appears out of nowhere, and befriends us like no other. Then he persists in moving along the search, 'without any personal interest or gains.' The whole situation lands him in the perfect position to stay *au courant* with all of the developments, without once arousing suspicion. Finally, he disappears when everything falls into place. Coincidentally, the falcon also departs, without any sign of forced entry into the suite."

"I know it sounds conclusive, but I would like to call it circumstantial evidence, and hope that you do too. Surely you haven't forgotten how the masterminds behind all of this are experts at framing people—with you and I being classic examples."

"Frankly, in my case, framing could only hold water if I believed in your explanations. Otherwise, everything appears fairly straightforward, with you at its core. Everything except your presence here, that is."

"You're hopeless, Jake Alexander! I don't understand why I even bother with you."

Samantha got up from her chair and started to make her way out of Jake's room *and* his life. But he grabbed her hand and pleaded with her to stay. He needed her for his survival—at least for now.

Samantha decided to help him, despite his unattractive insolence. It was important she clear her debt to him before moving on with her life—a life in which she had sworn off *all* men.

Another day clicked by—this time without stirring any urgency within Samantha, since the decision regarding the sultan had already been made.

As Sam and Jake sat in his convalescent room, theorizing, sarcasm and innuendoes continued to play an integral part in their soured-beyond-repair relationship. But they persisted, nonetheless. They had to. Their lives depended upon their ability to discern the truth.

The aimless shots in the dark were finally illuminated somewhat when a size sixteen nursing uniform strutted into Jake's room. A surgical mask disguised its occupant's face and the voice that muffled through.

"Thank you for finding our ring. We're sorry you had to get hurt in the process. But you put up quite the struggle—wanting to keep for yourself what you were to find for us. The enraged guard knifed you as a last resort, since his instructions were to not return empty-handed. You're lucky he didn't kill you! I can't imagine what inspired you to play such a deadly game."

"Look, lady, I don't know who the hell you are, or who you represent, for that matter. But I wasn't going to just hand over the ring to parties unknown.

Our lives depended upon proper submission."

"Let me assure you, everything is in order now. Thanks to you, the royal wedding will take place as planned—one week from today. Obviously, you two are invited, for without you, none of this could have come about."

The bearer of the news, with her English accent, wafted out of the room as quickly as she had wafted in—leaving Samantha and Jake perplexed. The signet ring drama appeared to have turned out appropriately, after all. And as a by-product, Sam and Jake were able to clear their minds of mutual suspicion. But where exactly did all of this leave greedy Sharon and her threat to their lives? And where was Feroz?

CHAPTER TWENTY-THREE

Three days before the imperial wedding, a messenger visited the medical center, bearing gifts for Sam and Jake. Included were a slew of extravagant garments, fit for a royal wedding; twenty-four-carat gold jewelry; precious stones and gems; two exclusive invitations to the four-day event; and of course, a prepaid hospital bill. Sam and Jake witnessed the calm with which everything was moving—both with respect to the wedding as well as their personal safety. The recovery of the ring had been advertised far and wide for over six days—confirming they no longer had possession of it. Samantha thought surely Sharon and whoever else was involved must have found that out by now. If someone wanted to come after them, they would have already made their move, as pointless as it would have been.

Almost everything seemed to have fallen into place—all except the missing falcon and the evanescent Feroz Khan. Neither Sam nor Jake could begin to guess what might have happened to him. Although he didn't appear to be involved in the assault on Jake, or any of the other stately events for that matter, nothing had made him exempt from stealing the falcon. Jake expressed rage at the thought of Feroz risking their lives, had they not found the other bargaining chip. He told Sam that he needed to know if their friend was a crook or a victim. He was prepared to extend his sleuthing abilities to finding him. However, raw knife wounds, fractured ribs and a broken jaw stopped him dead in his tracks before he could comfortably make his way out of his bed. Jake sat back down, with his head cradled in his palms, cursing the fierce pain that stung through him. Sam noticed the grimace on his face in response to the slightest movements. It was clear that the only way they could locate Feroz was through the police. A formal report was filed to get the wheels in motion.

The countdown to the royal ceremony started forty-eight hours prior to the actual event, with activities planned back to back. Sam was pleased that Jake had shown a remarkable recovery and was well enough to attend.

The first day began with *jaya mala*—a formal acceptance of the wedding by the bride and groom, designated by mutual outfitting with garlands. Samantha was touched that *both* the bride *and* the groom had their faces covered by veils made out of floral strands.

Having officially launched the ceremonies, Shanti and Ranjit were taken their separate ways, to be prepared by the women and the men, respectively.

Henna patterns were stained into the hands of all ladies present, but scented herbs and spices were saved exclusively for smoothing and purifying the bride's skin. A public bath followed, to show her unblemished epidermis as a testimonial for "unmarred goods"—safeguarding her against possible future abuse.

The groom also underwent preparation for his bride, although his focus leaned heavily in merrymaking, not beautification.

The infamous bath was concluded by a feast, marking the opening of contracts. A respected accountant kept a ledger of goods and moneys given by various families. They were to match gifts given them in the past—with inflation—and were to be reciprocated in a similar fashion in the future. Fair dealings and dowry were settled, with the Choudhrys and the Ranas contributing their appropriate allotments.

The day of the actual ceremony arrived. Shahnai music started to play at the crack of dawn, announcing the big event. Microphones amplified joyous songs throughout the community. Traffic was prohibited from entering the neighboring streets, cloistered by colorful tents known as *shamiyanas*, to create additional space. Caterers continued taking care of all meals for the two households, their guests and the *barat*—groom's processional—consisting of live bands, friends, relatives, acquaintances, horses, dancers, *hijdahs*, entertainers...

As the sounds of the big day made their way into Shanti's room, she trembled. Her body glistened with an anxious perspiration, while her heart felt dull with ache for Norman. She had pledged to give herself in humble submission exclusively to him, her one and only love. But here she was, preparing her virginity as a fruit for Ranjit. It disgusted her to marry where her heart wasn't. But she had to save her creed, by selling out to her "suitable" boy.

Looking into the mirror, Shanti mouthed, "You may have my body, Ranjit, but I will never surrender my soul to you. My spirit will forever belong to myself, and to my dear Norman. I'll marry you only for the sake of the people who breathed life into me. I must save them, and trust that my good karma will reunite me with my Norman in our next life—hopefully unbound by the limitations of rank and status. My only regret is that you innocently got caught in the middle of all this."

Shanti's diatribe was terminated by a throng of chirpy friends and handmaidens. They bore trays of flowers and heady incense, with smoke curling and rising like a cobra at a flute show. The team had congregated to help the chosen "lucky" girl get ready.

Shanti's shaking body was wrapped in a beautiful red and gold saree, with her midriff exposed. *Churrah,* a special arrangement of bridal bangles— to be removed only at the time of the announcement of the first pregnancy—was intermingled with other bangles, to cover the entire length of her forearm. Five rings adorned the fingers on each hand, with bejeweled chains extending into a bracelet. A *navaratna* medallion swung down onto her forehead, with tear drop pearls jingling off its lower border. Matching earrings danced from her ears. The set was completed with a complementary necklace, creating a miniature lacy garden on her slender, long neck. As a final touch, lips and nails were stained a vibrant red, eyes were accentuated in smoky gray, and dotted patterns in an array of colors were painted on her forehead.

Physically, the bride looked as radiantly beautiful and ready as was humanly possible. Emotionally...

At nightfall, Shanti peeked out of her window and saw Ranjit make his final entrance into the courtyard, prepared for the reveling. Though out of doors, the area was almost completely covered with a decorative ceiling of floral garlands, lights, metallic streamers and a constant sparkle of fireworks and stars twinkling through.

As the groom waited in his pink turban and floral veil by the holy fire that was to meld him to his bride, Shanti tremulously walked toward him. Following the initial prayers, she followed her lord and master around the fire seven times, representing the seven promises: devotion to each other;

praying for each other's happiness; being a help-mate in every worthy cause; being ever full of joy for each other; serving others together; following vows to each other throughout life; and living as best friends, treating each other as sovereign lords and gurus.

Although the male supremacy bothered Samantha, tears welled in her eyes in response to the touching pledges. The ceremony further warmed her heart when she learned the emphasis on respect for the female: a mother that bares all good things in life, one who has the exclusive gift to change seed to fruit and one who has the knowledge and wisdom to rule diligently, be it an empire or a household.

Samantha's face started to feel warm and flushed as the sultan reentered her thinking— making her yearn for being cherished by a soulmate, right into the days of faded beauty, silvering hair and fading wisdom.

But while she delighted in her choices, her heart couldn't help but cry out for Shanti—for behind the heavily embroidered veil was a bride stripped of her freedom of choice. Tears of constraint replaced nuptial glow. Not a single soul in attendance could hear the silent screams of the liquid diamonds that squealed their way out of the beautiful cat eyes.

After an entire night of liturgy, the deed was finally completed. Symbolically, the morning sun started its ascent in the east, signifying a new beginning. But dark clouds wrestled down its warm bright rays, sheathing everything in sight with a disheartening gray. Their fierce power was felt through the strong, whistling winds that forcefully shook and stirred. Branches fell to the ground as trees were dismembered. Rubbish cycloned around like a tornado, sucking up everything into its vortex. Mothers secured their young from the effects of the angry sandstorm. Dust dervishes spun and blew into the eyes of the wedding guests, closing them to the angry forces of destruction. Even Norman couldn't have planned it better.

But amidst all the savage desolation, two dynasties rejoiced at the *fait accompli,* a groom awaited to claim his bride, and a tall robust figure approached Samantha.

But before Sam could recognize the advancing glorious form, Jake grabbed her arm and insisted they take shelter. One look at his injuries and Samantha obliged.

Whether it was the storm or their rapid exit, the divine being lost track of Sam, even though his unrelenting gaze had born into her for the last hour. Disappointed as he was, he did not despair. He knew the separation was only temporary. He hadn't waited all this time to be discouraged by a minor setback.

Back at the hotel, Samantha was stunned at Jake's change of heart. For the very first time he seemed genuinely interested in her, *without* conjecture. She ventured a guess to herself that it was a corollary from being immersed in an intense emotional atmosphere, emphasizing the importance of family. Dying alone without kin was enough incentive to shake up just about anyone. But this once his timing was unsuitable to her for several reasons—being officially married, for one.

The sandstorm persisted for several additional hours, seeing to it that Samantha had no way out of Jake's uncomfortable presence. The twosome was definitely sequestered in the shelter of their hotel suite. And as if that wasn't bad enough, the tumult claimed the power that fed every form of solo entertainment—from reading lights to television and radio. All that was left was a good, old-fashioned, candlelight heart to heart.

Jake's ardor appeared to return as he became aware of their solitary confinement. His gaze perused the span of Samantha's body like a predator sizing up his prey. He looked, acted and sounded like a cliché. "Alone at last!"

Sam wasn't the least bit thrilled at him catching up to her, since she had already mourned and buried her feelings for him. But then came the wholehearted seduction, pouring out an irresistible incantation that even *she* was compelled to take notice of.

As Samantha reclined languorously in a thin cheesecloth sundress, Jake insinuated himself on the already occupied couch—right beside the lanky legs that covered its entire length. One foot at a time, he treated her to a massage that was relaxing, invigorating and sensual. According to him, it was something he had taken great pains to learn, under the tutelage of a guru who believed the foot was the center of all well-being and arousal—contrary to his own medical training. With each circular motion, Samantha's defenses melted away, converting her every individual muscle into a desiring piece of flesh. Jake looked at her aroused state and walked his fingers across the expanse he had just lured under his spell, all the way up to her tense temples. With the right pressure and movement, they, too, gave in. A moan escaped Samantha as she threw her head back. The undulating movement through her torso thrust her plump bosom near Jake's panting breath, begging for his attention. Jake blew on the engorged thimble-like structures at the two crests—stretching the thin material of her dress like cellophane. With every ounce of willpower she could muster, Samantha pulled away from the inevitable and sat up straight, like a celibate monk. But the raw scent of desire emerging from her defied her. The harder she tried to refuse, the harder Jake tried to seduce her—mind, body and soul. The moment finally came when she could no longer deny herself. But the carnal acts had to follow *her* cravings, not his.

Samantha partially undressed—slipping down her bodice and hiking up her skirt—leaving a disheveled mess of fabric around her waist. She wanted to present her breasts for stimulation, while exposing her erogenous zone to a dance of total indulgence.

"You want 'just sex,' Jake Alexander? Brace yourself, because that is *all* you'll get. And I can assure you, it will be the most dynamite 'just sex' at that."

Jake looked stunned, perplexed and uneasy. For the first time in his life, he appeared to be at a loss for words. The sense of control and intimidation excited Sam. It felt good to be in the driver's seat.

Without a moment's hesitation, Samantha placed Jake's hands on her breasts and coached him into stimulating her the way she enjoyed most. Next, she removed his pants, leaving the remainder of him fully clothed. One look and she was certain he was turned on by her dominance—for his erection stood harder than ever, pointing straight up at the ceiling. Samantha lowered herself to the floor, and pulled Jake beside her. They faced each other. Her hand took command of his firm shaft and rubbed it diligently against her enflamed pearl. On and on she went, delighting in sensations that gave her abounding gratification, driving Jake crazy.

One final rotation—and all voluntary control left her body. Her pleasure center spasmed, leaving her legs fluctuating between quaking and stiffness. Her limbs opened up and dropped lax by her sides like a rag doll. Jake looked at her helpless and desirable form and slid his sweaty body over hers, driving his cock into her. The stimulation was more than she could take. She threw her legs straight up into the air, engulfing him deeper into herself. On and on Jake went, swishing flesh against flesh, hearing Sam confess her most delicious and naughtiest thoughts, until...

CHAPTER TWENTY-FOUR

The rain that had finally settled the sandstorm stopped its lulling pitter-patter out of reverence to the full moon. Everything smelled fresh and clean. The drab gray hue of the day was whipped away by a radiant silvery glow of nightfall. Samantha walked out onto her hotel balcony to watch the moon bathe the entire city with its soothing milk-like beams. It looked every bit as beautiful and mysterious as her last night with the sultan—before he informed her of his final return. Samantha inhaled the fresh jasmine scent from the vine that graced her terrace and thought of the beautiful gardens she could have reigned over. But it all appeared to be immaterial now. Today was the deadline—with the sultan having no way of locating her. She had deliberately lost touch with him, out of fear of his omnipotent effect on her.

Samantha disappointedly shrugged her shoulders and walked back in. The long, flowing sheers in the doorway separated her fantasy world from reality. And reality it was—for Jake's contemplations filled the room with doom and gloom. Samantha caught his melancholy face in the flickers of lightning, freezing each expression into a strobe-like frame.

She wondered if he was back to believing that she had indeed handed over the falcon to an accomplice willingly, and then played her Ms. Innocent game for some inexplicable reasons. His theory around her guilt was just as preposterous as the explanation he offered for his own innocence—in the solo ring recovery—hinging primarily on an anonymous phone call. According to Jake, an informant clued him in to the disappearance of the falcon, leading him to secure the only other item that could be used as a barter for his life. Having found it, he refused its surrender in the face of being beaten almost to the point of death. None of it made any sense, especially not his heroics—jeopardizing the very life he was supposedly trying to save—unless they somehow involved concern for *her* life and safety.

Not wishing to open up the proverbial can of worms, Sammy decided to curl up with a book since the electricity was functioning once again. Her gaze was transfixed on the same word for about an hour, but her mind traveled the continents and back, trying to make sense of the missing falcon and the missing Mr. Khan.

Being detached from the here and now, Samantha jumped up with a start when the phone rang, deafeningly near her ear. It felt like a blaring echo through a hollow tunnel somewhere in a nightmare. Reflexively, her left hand spread across her chest, securing her heart from jumping out of her ribcage, while her right hand grabbed the offensive medium.

A timid voice made its way around the lump in Sam's throat as she barely whispered a hello. It was as if she was already expecting the shocking news that she was about to hear.

Not one more sound emerged from Sam's lips as she listened intently. Putting the receiver back on its cradle, Sam wondered how she would find the words to share the information with Jake. Every fiber in her hoped he wouldn't inquire, at least until she could get to the bottom of it and free Feroz from what appeared to be serious blame. But that was just wishful thinking.

With raised brows and gaping eyes, Jake inquired, "Well?"

"Well, what?"

"Well, what was that all about?"

"Oh that. That was just the police. They might have a lead for us. But...ehm...it's not substantial or conclusive enough to surmise."

"Why don't you let *me* be the judge of that."

"In all fairness to Feroz, I'd rather not disclose anything yet."

"Look, Sam, I've been really patient. But I need to know what our friend was up to—especially if he was the one responsible for endangering our lives."

Samantha ignored Jake's statement. She could see that he was already taking a judgmental attitude, without having heard the worst of it.

Her silence appeared to infuriate Jake. He raised his voice and shouted, "What I can't seem to understand is that for some reason you are *still* trying to protect him. I'd like to know why that is—along with everything else you've learned."

Rage flamed out of Sam's indignant eyes as she puckered them into barely open horizontal slits. With flared nostrils and lips drawn into a snarl, she yelled, "How *dare you* start that again, after having made love to me less than two hours ago? And don't even think about blaming this one on Sharon, her swami, hypnosis, frame-up, or Feroz, for that matter! I'm tired of you jumping to conclusions, never giving anyone the benefit of the doubt—and to top that, having the gall to use everyone as your scapegoats."

"I think the only way we will survive this game is if we never again keep anything from each other."

"I'll agree to that, but only under one condition. You are no longer to hang anyone—not without a fair trial and a complete look at the evidence."

Jake reached out his beefy paw and shook Sam's hand.

"The police reported that Feroz was last seen in India the day after he left us, while boarding a plane to Queens, Canada. His photograph has been faxed to the authorities there, but they haven't heard anything yet." Samantha hesitated, gestured as if to be changing her mind, but then continued, "Well, actually, that isn't entirely true. An *unconfirmed* report has indicated that he might have been in touch with your ex-wife, Sharon."

"I knew it. He was working with her all along. How ingenious—to have established contact with us as our friend, only to access our information, while nudging us to move along."

"There you go again. I'm sorry to have opened my mouth."

With arms half-raised, palms opened out and volume decreased a couple of notches, Jake said, "I apologize. But you have to admit, even you can't come up with any other viable explanations for this one."

Samantha chose not to acknowledge Jake's statement. With downcast eyes, she herself was beginning to second-guess Feroz.

Samantha's disappointment drove deeper than Jake's, since it went beyond being let down by a friend. She had seriously considered allowing Feroz a chance to pursue her—seeing him as more loyal than Jake and less intimidating than the sultan.

The deadly silence was interrupted by Jake's take-charge voice. "Since we don't seem to have anything else that is keeping us here, I say we take the next flight out to Queens. I need to make *whoever* is responsible for putting us through hell pay for it."

Quietly and quickly, Sam and Jake packed up,

cleared their bill, and headed out to the Indira Gandhi International Airport.

The drive to the airport symbolized an exit from a country they had both grown to love and enjoy, despite their precarious quandary. Samantha took a deep breath to inhale the hot air, thick with aromas and memories. The smell of delicate spices that permeated the air outside of restaurants burst saliva out of her taste buds. Her gaze traveled over the colorful life all about her as she absorbed it into her memory, one last time. And finally the distinctive sounds that she had learned to distinguish amidst perpetual pandemonium warmed her heart like the melody from a favorite song. Truly, the Far East had seduced her, in every way imaginable.

Samantha cried softly as the 747 took off. India disappeared below, devoid of its characteristic colors.

Samantha stared blankly out her window, thinking about all the options she had walked away from. The one that stood most impressionably above the rest, especially now, was the mesmerizing sultan. But quite apart from her suitors and her crises, she felt she was leaving behind a big part of her heart in India. Samantha knew that things would never be the same without it. She was definitely going to miss the ways, the pace, the adventure and the constant surge of sensuality that she had grown accustomed to.

Taking life's inventory wasn't restricted just to Samantha. Jake also reviewed the last few months of his life. They ran like a movie in his mind, reaffirming his fondness for Sam. Jake knew that no woman with a banal life could ever satisfy him like her—she had survived bizarre experiences, with and without him. But while he knew that, he feared he had already alienated her once too often, even through his brave and loving gestures, by not owning up to them. Only some big force of nature could move her to him now, intertwining their lives once again.

The plane finally made its decent into Queens, Canada. A secured corridor funneled the passengers into the main terminal. Although the stifling lifeless hallway was closed, with nothing but drab fluorescent lights dressing it, Samantha could feel the cool air outside. It was quite different from the heat she had left behind—originally in Queens, and more recently in India. The short and crisp summer was definitely over in her country, but the exploit that started it all still awaited its dramatic conclusion.

Sam and Jake had barely cleared customs and immigration when a detective accosted them. Attempting a disgruntled handshake and flashing his badge, he introduced himself.

"Hi, I'm Detective Johnston. I've been working with the police in India, in connection with locating a valuable curio that was smuggled out recently. Such pieces are not to leave the country under any circumstances—not even with their proprietors. But we located a deal going down. The rarity in question was being traded for something. The smuggler swears it was a matter of life and death, and that he had every intention of returning it once he had guaranteed his goal. Needless to say, the police do not buy such stories and have every intention of prosecuting. But in order to indict the criminal, we need to first contact the rightful owners of the relic. And from what I understand, you two have been named as such—which brings us to our next point. We need to establish the facts around your involvement in the smuggling, to decide what to do with you. Finally, if you do get released from this one, we will still need to hand you over to homicide. They've been waiting for you for months now, to question you about the Norman Fairchild case."

Jake smashed his hand into a nearby concrete pole, expressing his fury. "Damn Feroz! How could he have been so stupid?"

"Stupid has nothing to do with it, Jake. He would have easily pulled it off, if it wasn't for us tipping off the police. I bet you they think we were in on it together—and being double-crossed, we blew the whistle on him."

"Bingo!" grimaced Detective Johnston.

Samantha and Jake were escorted to the police headquarters, luggage and all, directly from the airport. Upon their arrival there, they were ushered to an interrogation room, right past shouting offenders claiming innocence. To Sam and Jake, they looked undeniably like criminals. *Just as they themselves must appear to the officials*, thought Sam.

Through the half-open venetian blinds shielding the back room window, Sam identified the familiar handsome face that had "befriended" them many moons ago.

As the door opened to reunite the threesome, Feroz's face lit up with assurance. But Samantha sneered at him with contempt. Feroz gathered that she was disillusioned with him, not yet having ascertained that he risked life and limb for her. Fear overtook him as he realized that his last source of hope was undoubtedly about to forsake him. And then there was Jake. With a total lack of self-control, the irate hulk lunged for the prisoner being held despite his innocence.

Trying to exonerate himself, Feroz shouted, "I can explain everything! I have it on tape! I didn't want to hand it over until I had you guys as my witnesses—just in case Sharon had connections higher up."

To conclude the monologue that no one paid heed to, Feroz reached his right hand into his right pocket, to "defend" himself. But before he could draw the "defense weapon," two others were drawn out at him, claiming his life with six gunshot wounds. Feroz's body slid down along the desk he was leaning against—sticky, bright red streaks marking his last voyage—as he struggled to gasp for his last few breaths. Surrounding him was a pool of his lifeblood—abandoning him in his hour of need—just like those about him. All present were speckled in the blood that had sustained his innocuous life a few moments ago.

But it was all a big, irreparable mistake. Feroz's defense weapon was a mere audio tape, not intended to hurt anyone other than the actual perpetrators behind the heinous crimes.

CHAPTER TWENTY-FIVE

The die had been cast. Mortality started its decisive motion, predestined to flow like running water. No one could stop it or change its course.

Time stood still, with each second hanging like an hour. The rescue mission moved in slow motion, while thoughts raced like a whirlwind.

Sam shrieked with cries of horror. Watching the irreversible extraction of life in cold blood was more than she could stomach. The finality, the pointlessness, and the anticipated delivery of the news to Feroz's hospitable family flashed through her mind like a ghastly nightmare. Sam wished that she could believe in reincarnation, knowing that Feroz's good karma would land him in a happier life next time around. He had certainly paid many times over for the pain he had caused Anita. But as hard as Sam tried, nothing could absolve her from the guilt of not believing in the man who always believed in her, without questions or exceptions.

Following the futile rescue attempt, Feroz's body was wheeled out, right past Samantha. She wanted to wrap herself around him, breathing her own breath into him, reviving him and begging him for his forgiveness. But the empty shell was torn away from her, despite her pleas and helpless screams.

Jake tried his best to comfort Sam, by supporting her shoulders in his firm embrace. But she shrugged off his hands with repugnance—for she could smell the death and blame on them.

Losing the sanity within herself, Samantha used her own hands to pounce at Jake's throat, yelling, "Murderer," for it was his insinuations, his innuendoes, his report and his mistrust that had caused the firing of the murder weapons.

Samantha's hysterics didn't help Jake one iota. He was immediately taken into custody, while she herself was taken aside for questioning, despite the pain that plagued her. Sam's speech became incoherent from the sobs and screams that punctuated it. Lucky for her, the display bought her time. But it also had a downside—something she hadn't expected.

Samantha had a chance to listen to the lethal tape. It began by disclosing the reason for Feroz's sudden visit to Sharon. Seeing the turmoil that Sam's life was in, with no hopeful way out, Feroz had decided to take things into his own hands— solving the mystery that robbed her of her freedom and her safety. Feroz's plan involved a meeting with Sharon, designed to trick her into a complete confession, using his ingenious methodology and the falcon—the irresistible bate. The information was to free Sam and Jake from any form of culpability and remove the threat to their lives by having the real executors of the macabre crimes arrested and thrown behind bars. The tape also covered the details of Feroz's undercover role and procedures, to avoid the possibility of misplaced blame on him.

Feroz outlined that he was to approach Sharon and disclose his knowledge of her interest in the signet ring, as sensed through Norman's notes. Posing as Jake's and Sam's fellow expeditionary, he was to convince her that although they couldn't find the ring, they had located, during their search, a valuable falcon—far more precious than the ring itself. But despite him being instrumental in finding the priceless piece, he had not been fairly rewarded. He was thereby hoping to sell her the falcon himself—to get his "fair" share.

Next, having heard of Sharon's narcissistic ego, he was going to flatter her regarding her brave tactics and brilliant strategies—hoping to unravel her devious *modus operandi* in all of its boastful glory. Woven through would be the plea to not do away with his teammates, to watch them squirm—since he was certain he had enough to keep their mouths shut, making them non-threatening. Feroz intended to stand firm in demanding the disclosure of the juicy workings, *before* trading the rare smuggled curio. He was going to impress upon her that he wasn't one to conduct business without first being excited by the bravado of his partner in crime. Feroz planned to get a comprehensive account, baiting her with whatever was necessary—flattery, unspoken threats, intimidation, volunteering bits of information...

As the grand finale, he was only going to show her one half of the falcon, making it clear the remainder would be somehow sent from India, *after* he had received his money and returned home to safety. Initially, it was to guarantee him his life, in light of his goods and his pompous attitude. Eventually, it was crucial in buying the time he would need to have her arrested.

The tape then switched over to the actual meeting with Sharon. It revealed, in reality, that the plan didn't go quite as smoothly.

As one might have expected, Sharon's swami tried to overpower Feroz, to forcefully claim the falcon, and to rid them of loose ends. Feroz informed him that he wasn't stupid enough to bring the entire piece with him. Swami wanted to kill him, but Sharon insisted on checking his wares first. Luckily for Feroz, the half-falcon technique worked—because without its counterpart, it was worthless.

Having established the upper hand, Feroz began the negotiations. But his terms for wanting to be "impressed" with a complete account were denied, hands down. Feroz persisted in wanting to do business his way—skillfully bringing in some blackmail. He threatened to go to the police with what little he knew—making it stick by planting the right "evidence"—unless they could come up with a viable solution in his favor. Feroz impressed upon them the fact that he wasn't one to lose. Having the power to control someone's fate, especially those who didn't play his game, was far more delicious to him than fame and fortune. His smugness hinged on his knowledge that killing him at that point would be counterproductive, since he dangled the goods in front of the addict's eyes—breaking down her defenses. Samantha could just see him chuckle to himself, amazed at how crooks tend to place far too much faith in other crooks, never once thinking that one of the unprincipled breed could turn on them at any time. It was clear that when one is driven by greed, anything is possible.

What followed was right on target. Sam could practically feel Sharon's soulless eyes and malign expression as she began disclosing the disgraceful account of all that had transpired in her shrilling, arrogant, remorseless voice.

Sharon indicated that it all had started when she met Allen, quite accidentally, at an East Indian art auction shortly after her separation from Jake. Raging hormones and chemistry took over their conversation right from the outset. It was obvious he wanted her, just as much as she wanted him. Allen did the male thing and began trying to impress her with whatever he could. At first, she snickered at his complete lack of knowledge as far as art was concerned. But then, something happened. Allen realized that she saw right through him and brought out his trump card to save face. He began talking about a rare piece, aged beyond anything she had ever held in her curator's hands, worth millions. Naturally, it grabbed more than her attention. Instantly, she inquired all that she could, with dreamy school-girl fascination, appealing to Allen's male ego. The more she learned, the more she became convinced that the two lugs could be talked out of giving it up if the right offer was made. In time, she managed to convince her poor lover to talk Norman into selling out. She told him the piece belonged in a museum. But as hard as Allen tried to pressure Norman into selling the "useless" item, to generate an obscene amount of money that would set them both for life, Norman didn't budge. He was more interested in avenging his biological mother's death, using the falcon as proof of his lineage. No amount of money could have talked him out of his obsession. The disagreement poisoned the relationship between the two best friends, with her pulling away at the strings—for all the good it did.

Not achieving her desired results, she got more aggressive. Unbeknownst to Allen, she tampered with Norman's brakes, in hopes of putting him out of commission—leaving Allen in charge of the information she needed to locate the valuable treasure. Unfortunately, Allen drove along, sacrificing his own life. Norman was still alive but incapacitated.

Having no other choice at the time, she started pressuring Norman directly. But, as before, he persisted in his stubbornness. It was time for a new strategy.

Knowing that it was over between herself and Jake, with him showing a total lack of respect for her work, she decided to use him as a pawn in her game. It was perfect. He wasn't one to tolerate loneliness for too long, and Samantha was just his type—someone he could easily fall for. Once they were coupled, pushing the right buttons could scare them into getting her anything she wanted. Sharon emphasized that it was the most delicious part of her ploy, since the means were just as mouthwatering as the ends.

Mind games and hypnosis were utilized, eventually bringing Jake and Sam together, as planned. Not wishing to waste any time, she arranged to have their picture taken at their very first meeting—just in case...

Next, swami and she paid Norman one final visit. They had hoped to scare him into cooperation with their latest scheme, showing him the picture as proof of them meaning business; however, Norman persisted in his silent, obstinate ways— leading them to switch to plan B.

Plan B entailed suffocating Norman, with Jake and Sam set up to take the blame. The latter was ensured by sending their photograph to the papers, concocting a phony back-dated life insurance policy as motive, and tipping the police anonymously. The noose was further tightened by the planting of an unregistered gun on Sam, unnerving her through a violation of her property, and the timely riddance of their cumbersome accomplice, Robin Hutton. According to Mr. Hutton, he was to get Sam and Jake to his office to "encourage" them into their mission. But the real agenda was merely to land them at the site of the second murder, executed by the previously planted but currently missing weapon. The deadly combination of events was enough to scare anyone into running while they could.

Sharon fully expected that in a matter of time they would find the falcon—which was what she had wanted all along—and return to Queens. Its recovery was to be as uncomplicated as her helping herself to Jake's apartment, without anyone ever knowing about it.

Everything was looking good—that is, until Sam and Jake stumbled upon the wrong clue, thinking the search involved the signet ring. In reality, the ring was nothing more than a red herring that gained a momentum all its own—attracting new, unrelated parties—throwing them off course.

After a long wait, with obstacles beyond her control, Sharon wanted to give up—seeing that her drive had lost its flavor since she could no longer witness her power over life and death. She would never have gone to India, even for that. She hated the thought of heat and smog. But then Feroz showed up with the piece in question, ready to sell out.

Sharon's thrilled voice climaxed with, "How perfect! How wo-o-onderful! How absolutely unbelievable!" Her tone flaunted a total lack of contrition toward the hideous crimes she had just revealed. It was obvious she went to extremes to get what she wanted. And what she desired earnestly was to get her hands on the object that would give her prominence overnight—though not through the museum, as she had led Allen to believe. No, Sharon's fame was to come through personal fortune, after privately auctioning the rare falcon.

Following that disclosure, the deed was completed. The half falcon was exchanged for half the money and a guarantee to spare Feroz, Jake and Sam's lives. Knowing the latter was insured only until the promised time of delivery of the second half of the falcon, Feroz wanted the abominable creatures arrested as quickly as possible—prior to arousing suspicions—restoring all goods and order.

Sam realized it was at that point that he was arrested, with herself and Jake tipping off the police—just as he was about to return with the good news to India, along with the reassurance that the signet was a separate, non-life-threatening issue. "And the rest," she said, "became history."

Feroz's taped voice gripped at Samantha. It was as real as if he were standing right there—alive and well. His wisdom, love, loyalty and concern shone right through his message. Nothing that Sam had experienced before could ever compare to the pain she felt right then. But that wasn't the worst part—for she knew it would haunt her forever. Such scars were not meant to be healed in time, with proper grieving. Life couldn't just go on with the justification that the deceased would have wanted it that way.

Samantha wanted to curse and swear, but she didn't know what she could say... Damn Norman? Damn Jake? Damn Sharon? Damn herself? *Damn! Damn! Damn!*

Epilogue

Sam's life completed yet another circle, bringing her back to a cemetery for a third time, laying another one of her loved ones to rest—all thanks to Sharon. She wanted to rip out the cold heart that claimed all those close to her, but all she could do was hope that the Queen of Death and Destruction—the black widow—would taste a fate worse than death in poverty, humiliation and captivity.

The ceremony began with sharp cries and screams piercing through in a language Samantha didn't understand. Blaming stares whipped away at her numb body, reviving her pain with a jolting jumpstart. Nobody understood her genuine grief. Nobody.

At the conclusion, Samantha stood alone in black raiment, while a parade of attendants walked by in white, the mourning color that expresses the desire to send the deceased to the purity of heaven—something she learned when it was too late. One by one they spat at her, expressing their disgust, dismay and disdain. But through it all, Sam stood still, not daring to move or defend herself. She felt truly deserving of the hostility aimed at her.

Once all was said and done, with everyone gone, Samantha moved closer to Feroz's grave, wanting to pay her last respects. Uncontrolled cries burst out for the great man she had brought back for proper burial among his own. It was the least she could do, realizing how horrible it felt to lay Norman to rest away from his people. But nothing she did could make her feel any better. Her guilt, pain, and shame were beyond consolation.

For hours, Samantha kneeled and wept in repentance. The mysterious man who watched her lamenting didn't dare disturb her. He had waited to catch up with her since the day of the royal wedding, and an entire lunar cycle before then. A few additional moments were certainly not going to hurt.

Samantha finally rose from the ground, ready to leave the country that had brought her the most memorable of experiences, both good and bad. She had to leave, because lingering would be too painful now. Besides, what did she really have left to linger for? If she were to stay, she would become nothing more than a statistic one day. Someone dying alone, just as Norman had, away from his people.

But as she turned around, wiping the sting of tears from her eyes, a familiar silhouette approached her with out-stretched arms, wanting to take her into the shelter of his omnipotent embrace.

"Come to me, my beautiful wife, and allow me to take away your pain. You are my responsibility, my life, my soulmate, and my love."

Samantha's fragile, disheveled form fainted right into his arms, oblivious to his identity, before she could take notice of the rapidly approaching horse and equestrian. Worry plagued the rider's face as he dismounted beside them. But then the incognizant lips mouthed, "I love you, Jake."

With tears in his eyes, the honorable sultan transferred the unconscious goddess into the arms she would most want to wake up in.

About The Author

Born in India, Rebecca Rosenblat immigrated to Canada at the age of sixteen, where she attended the University of Toronto and graduated with a Bachelor of Science in Psychology and Biology. As a Research Co-ordinator at the Clarke Institute of Psychiatry, She became a popular lecturer and was published in sword medical journals before deciding to pursue her love of fiction. Ms.Rosenblat currently resides in Toronto with her husband and two children.

A man and a woman, a mysterious stranger, a land of ancient culture, and signet ring that could mend a Royal Feud if it hadn't been stolen...

An Eastern Seduction

by
Rebecca Rosenblat
